Mrs. Hungerford

A Life's Remorse

Vol. I

Mrs. Hungerford

A Life's Remorse
Vol. I

ISBN/EAN: 9783337064457

Printed in Europe, USA, Canada, Australia, Japan

Cover: Foto ©Andreas Hilbeck / pixelio.de

More available books at **www.hansebooks.com**

A LIFE'S REMORSE.

A Novel.

BY THE AUTHOR OF

"MOLLY BAWN," "PHYLLIS," "UNDERCURRENTS,"
"THE HONBLE. MRS. VEREKER," &c., &c.

"To-morrow, and to-morrow, and to-morrow."

IN THREE VOLUMES.

VOL. I.

LONDON:

F. V. WHITE & CO.,

31, SOUTHAMPTON STREET, STRAND, W.C.

1890.

PRINTED BY
KELLY AND CO., MIDDLE MILL, KINGSTON-ON-THAMES;
AND GATE STREET, LINCOLN'S INN FIELDS, W.C.

TO

HELEN C. BLACK,

IN MEMORY OF

Y PLEASANT HOURS GIVEN TO ME
BY HER.

A LIFE'S REMORSE.

A LIFE'S REMORSE.

—✹—

PROLOGUE.

—✹—

CHAPTER I.

A SQUALID street, a dense crowd—swaying, angry, excited. All eyes seem fixed upon the door of one house, near which two policemen are standing, and from which every now and then men, evidently in authority, emerge. It is mid July, the 15th, and the glaring sun, though seen but dimly through the smoky London sky, is sending down its hot rays with such force that the air is terribly oppressive. Just here, in this dull side street, the heat is intolerable, yet nobody seems inclined to move on. Men, women and children stand watching the house with a morbid interest, talking loudly, unceasingly, and always with an under-growl of hopeful rage in their tones.

Last night a crime of no ordinary sort had been committed here. Behind the guarded doors the body of the victim is still lying. There is nothing in the outside of the house suggestive of anything out of the common; it is indeed as meagre as its fellows, as innocent of paint or whitewash, as miserably unacquainted with cleansing of any sort, but inside, as is well known to the watching crowd, it widely differs from Nos. 7 and 11. This No. 9 is indeed a gambling hell of the distinctly better sort, which young men belonging to the aristocracy, and young men desirous of belonging to it, have seen fit to patronize occasionally in sheer idleness of spirit, and that vague longing to do the thing forbidden that is as the breath of life to us, and was born with our common mother, Eve.

Just now a red shadow seems to rest upon the house; the surging angry crowd see it only through a flush of crimson that dyes it the colour of blood. The deep sunset is giving a helping hand to this ghastly fancy, and with wild gesticulation the roused populace of this unsavoury place (that yet is hardly a stone's-throw from fashionable quarters), converse together of last night's fatal occurrence.

To the mental vision, the form of the young girl lying in her shroud within the house of evil repute, is plain. She had been a very young girl, innocent of any connection with the gambling part of the concern; a daughter of one of the servants who attended there; a quite common girl, one of the people. There had been a raid upon the house, a hint had been given to the police; there had been a *mêlée*, a rush, and she, who had most unfortunately come there that night for the first time in her life to bring a message to her father—a message, said gossip, that ever delights to pile up the agony, about a dying brother—had been shot in the scuffle. She had been killed —by mistake, said some, but they were cried down upon; *malice prepense*, said others, and these had room given to them. She had been shot, and purposely, said the latter seers, having been suspected of treachery, and of having sold " them " to the police.

By " them " were meant the ordinary

1—2

habitués of the place; but there had been
present last night a large sprinkling of men
from the more select portion of society—men
whose reputation stood high in the social
world, and who would have risked a good
deal to keep their names out of the scandal
that must ensue on their discovery in such a
disreputable, if gilded, hole.

Some had been arrested on the spot, but the
greater number had, in the confusion of the
moment, escaped. Those captured were of
the baser metal, and to secure some whose
names would ring through England was now
felt by the police authorities to be the one
thing worth living for. *That* would drag the
affair into eminence. It would help effectually
to put down this disgrace to civilization that
stood within their midst.

The desire to arrest had been strong in the
breast of the force at all times, but when the
girl lay dead, shot to the heart, upon the
ground, with cards and dice strewn thick as
leaves in Vallambrosa round her, with the
blood rushing from her young bosom, and her
father, regardless of all consequences, kneeling

beside her, and calling aloud upon her name, a downright passionate thirst of blood broke out in the myrmidons of the law, and they sought to lay hands heavily on all men with a view to seeing justice done.

The girl was well known ; was popular. A pretty creature, prettier than ever now as she lay within her last coverings, with that terrible, beautiful, ineffable smile upon her young lips. The populace, ever prone to excitement of one kind or another, had risen in a body, desirous if possible to avenge her murder—certain at all events to make a sensation of it. It is easy at most times to move the people. They will cry for the death of a puppy, if told in tones sufficiently lachrymose, and will laugh at the death of a kitten if the narrator gives it to them in any truly witty vein. At this moment their most savage instincts are awake, and they wait upon the comings and goings of the servants of the law as though their own lives depend upon them.

Last night was Saturday ! And here is Sunday, a day well into the evening, and as yet no sure tidings of the real perpetrator of that fatal act has been gained. The people are growing impatient. They press more and more closely on the door, as if drawn to the fatal spot by some horrible fascination.

The police have been making inquiries right and left, but nothing coming of them the crowd is losing patience. Detectives, with a hurried, subdued whisper to the policeman guarding the door, push their way through the masses and disappear into the by streets at either side.

Suddenly, on the heels of one of these last, a tall man in official uniform steps into the dying sunlight. He is instantly recognized by the onlookers as one of those who last night had been most instrumental in arresting the visitors at the hell. He had had his face cut open in the affray, and now stands blinking in the light, with a huge white plaster drawn across his right cheek. The people watching him grow silent; he is standing on the top step of the flight that leads to the hall door of the ill-omened house, and is looking straight out before him as if lost in puzzled thought, a heavy frown upon his brow.

Suddenly this frown lightens, and his whole face springs into eager life. His eyes grow bright, intense, and fasten themselves with all the avidity of a beast of prey upon some object that stands back of the mass of human beings that are searching his face as though the desired knowledge for which they wait lies in it. He makes a step forward.

"That man! *Stop him!*" he cries in a clear ringing voice, extending his arm over the people to a direction that would lead to the left. Two or three people on the outskirts of the crowd turn, and know by a certain instinct that the slight, well-dressed, elegant-looking man behind them is the person held up to public scrutiny.

They have barely time to thus place their instincts, when the man, who is young and of a very agile build, and whose own instincts are apparently as acute as theirs, makes a movement to draw back from them. A fatal movement! In a second the crowd sways round—the attention of every one present is directed towards him—another moment, and the policeman's hand is on his shoulder, and a

dull roar, muffled as yet, but rich in promise
of sterner things to come, sounds within his
ears.

"You were here last night," says the man
with the gash upon his face. "I saw you. I
remember your face well."

"My good fellow, you are mistaken. If I
had been here last night, do you think I
should be here now?" says the gentleman in
a wonderfully even tone, but in his rather
forced smile there is fear.

"Most likely," says the policeman unmoved.
"They're often like that. They comes back
reglar. Come, you'd better give in; I'd swear
to you at any moment, and we're wanting
witnesses for this case."

"But I assure you," begins the other, always
with that calm manner but that unmanageable
smile, "that you are mistaken. I can prove
an alibi——" he looks sharply from right to
left. The people are crowding round him;
with his elbow he instinctively pushes back a
swarthy fellow who is pressing even closer.
A quick hunted look grows within his eyes;
escape seems impossible, and to be identified

with this scandalous affair—to have his name
dragged in—to——

It seems inevitable, however. With an inward groan he is about to acknowledge this,
when a sudden well-known sound, as of the
rapid approach of many horses, causes a panic
in the crowd. At the lower end of the street
a fire-engine comes into view, the horses tear
up the street, the people give way. Seeing in
a second his one chance of escape, the tall
man dashes the policeman against the wall
near him, and with a spring breaks through
the crush and darts down a side lane.

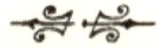

CHAPTER II.

HE is round the corner in a moment, the yelling crowd after him. His sudden flight from justice has removed all doubts as to his guilt, and, smelling blood, the men, women, and children pursue him.

On, on, now nearing him, now distanced as the prey puts on a fresh courage, they follow him ; he is now getting into a better part of the town, a solitary, half-asleep looking quarter, where the houses are more respectable, and shops fewer. He has turned a corner, with the sickening certainty that his breath is failing him, and that the hooting, hideous, revengeful pack behind are gaining on him.

For the moment he is out of sight; the friendly corner has hidden him. The street is utterly deserted so far as he can see, and as he glances with feverish eyes around him he becomes conscious of a hall door standing wide open. Mechanically he glances at it—10, Sandiford Street.

It is a last chance! Quick as lightning he springs inside the door ; it is a sudden impulse, born of no thought, and may mean but the last movement in the luckless game.

He is spent, however, and it *is* a chance, however poor. He is up the steps, and into this quiet house that seems to have opened out to him arms of salvation.

He is only just in time ; the yells of his pursuers tell him, as he stands panting in the tiny hall, that they are now in the street with him. Will they, or will they not, pass the door ?

Turning a handle on his right, he enters a small room, tastily furnished, and evidently the apartment of some bookish person. It is empty. Once inside it, with no possibility of getting out again unseen, a sense of maddening despair falls upon him, and with lips so tightened that the teeth show between them, he stands a human thing at bay ! Afterwards, he always told himself with a shuddering terror, yet a feeling of hope of absolution, that during those terrible moments of suspense he lost his brain, and was hardly to be considered accountable for anything he might have done.

Standing listening now in the empty little library, he waits on events, with pale face and brilliant eyes. Should it occur to one of those whooping idiots outside to do as he did, to turn into the open doorway that has given him sanctuary—what then? All will be at an end. Publicity inevitable! Guiltless as he is of last night's mournful crime, he was yet one of the gambling party, and his name will assuredly be made much of, in the examination of this hateful affair; it will appear in public print. His name! Hitherto so immaculate! His very soul grinds within him!

As for the girl, that poor child, he had had nothing to do with her death—he thanked God for that! It was not likely that an English gentleman would go out in the evening armed with a revolver. Her death lay at the door of—well, some foreigner very likely. But he had been present; he had even been so unfortunate as to see the girl come into the room, and heard her scream as a chance shot

hit her. It had been horrible—it had haunted
him—it had drawn him back to this place to-
day, and this lesser sensation, in which he is
now figuring, seems a part, an outcome, of the
whole. It is but natural that out of the great
storm other winds should arise.

It is unlucky, however, that *he* should be
the victim. He who has always held himself
so chin-high above his brethren. What devil
tempted him to go to that detestable hole last
night? The world, *his* world, regards him as
a Brutus, an honourable man indeed, and to
be cast down from his high estate would be
to him a catastrophe too bitter to be borne.
Death rather than that—*anything!*

Yet if these fools find him, a most unen-
viable notoriety must assuredly be his—an
even painful notoriety, in all possibility. The
populace, incensed as they are, would think
little of tearing him in pieces. An infuriated
mob is a bad thing to face, and this mob is
ripe for anything. Not that he shrinks from
its vengeance, however rough. Better death
than the disgraceful gossip that must ensue
upon discovery.

Discovery! The very word opens out a new
era to the man who up to this has been free of
fear of any sort. A man to whom the breath
of universal good opinion is as life itself. The
man to whom even saintly people have given
the hand of fellowship, and the *word*—which
means a good deal more.

His gifts of charity have been large and
various—so large as to call for flattering comment from the press; and—to do him justice
—were given in no grudging manner, and with
no poor desire to attract the world's attention,
but given heartily and because he honestly
wished to give. There was no pettiness
about him—no vicious tendency of any sort
—nothing to which one would point an
objecting hand—save, perhaps, a slight
savagery of disposition, and that was so
low-lying as to be unknown even to the
man himself.

He draws a deep breath, and involuntarily
takes a defensive attitude. The cries, the running feet, are at the door now; they pass.
The pack in full cry is racing round the next
corner, only a straggler or two following in its

wake is to be heard. The danger, whatever it was, is at an end.

With his hand clutching one of the velvet curtains of the window, he glances cautiously out, to draw back again presently with a sigh of relief. The surging crowd is gone. The quiet street takes on its usual sabbatical calm. It is over. His name—so dear to him—need not now be connected with this hideous affair. There is no more to fear. A heavy breath of self-gratulation parts his lips. He draws himself up to his full height, and turning to make his way homewards, finds himself face to face with another man.

A tall old man, bent, scholarly in appearance, with keen eyes that shine like stars in his withered face. A bookworm evidently; of venerable aspect, and of a sad countenance. A very old man, and one who had made long acquaintance with grief. His bright, strangely youthful eyes fix themselves upon the intruder, as if naturally to question the reason of his presence here, and having fixed themselves refuse to move, growing large indeed with comprehension half awake.

The latter, thus brought face to face with a fresh danger, collects himself sufficiently to stay the exclamation that had been upon his lips, and turns a countenance ghastly indeed, but composed, upon the owner of the house. With necessity for composure has come the power to show it.

"I have to beg your pardon, sir," says he, advancing a step or two towards the old man. "There was a commotion in the street outside —some wretched criminal, I fancy, having been detected in the act of picking a pocket. The crowd was pursuing him, and I——" he pauses here, and presses his hand to his side. "My heart is weak. I dread excitement of any kind. Finding your door open, I ventured to come in and take refuge here, until," smiling, "the storm should be overpast. There is no further danger of a jostling, I think, so," with a courteous bow, "I will rid you of an uninvited guest."

He makes another step forward, this time towards the door. But the old man, making a movement that checks his progress, holds out a threatening hand.

" A moment, sir," says he. " I was myself one of the crowd you speak of. I saw the ' wretched criminal '—I saw him sufficiently well," with a piercing glance, " to know that it was *you*."

" Stand back," says the younger man with a sudden fierceness.

" I refuse to let you stir until this matter is investigated," cries the other in shrill tones. " There shall be justice, sir, justice ! The death of that young girl shall not go un-avenged———"

" Stand back, I say," repeats the younger man in low dangerous tones.

" Stand back, *you*, sir. Any one connected with last night's infamous murder must be———"

He stops here with a thick gurgle, for the other's hand is on his throat. With a savage grasp that kills the cry that would have risen, he presses back the old man till he has him on his knees, and then upon his back, and then with a fierce passion he dashes the white head, once, twice, thrice, with horrible force against the floor.

CHAPTER III.

It might have been the work of half an hour, or half a minute. The younger man, rising, scarce knows which it is. He looks stealthily down upon his work. Hah! At least the old fool is still ; his tongue wags no more. It will take him time to recover consciousness—precious time, that will enable *him*, the assaulter, to escape. And what is an hour's relief from the worries of existence? Why nothing—a matter to be grateful for, no more. A deeper, sweeter sleep, because dreamless.

There is no movement in the shrunken body. He has fainted. How like a faint is to——. When people faint they are always pale; pale as——. Well, it was a pity he should have compelled him to faint, but it was the old man's own fault. He *would* have it—and——. Great Heaven! What horrid thing is that ?—that dark, dark, *red* spot, coming from under the nostril and trailing slowly down—slowly—slowly——

Stop it, some one! *stop it!* or it will enter the white, parted lips. Oh——!

He turns, and flies the room. Outside there is still a straggler or two rushing past, and, joining in with them, he runs too. These last are newcomers in the race, to whom his features are unfamiliar, and he runs with them in all safety, being indeed accepted by them as an ardent hankerer after justice.

And as he runs, he feels a certain joy in the quick movement, the swift rushing through the air! The very wings of Mercury seem lent to him. He seems to fly upon the wind. So fast he goes that he outstrips his companions, and carried away by this mad new spirit that possesses him, is in danger of coming up with those first enemies who would know him and decry him.

On a sudden he recollects that, pulls himself up abruptly, and taking advantage of a moment that leaves him free of suspicion, darts down a side street, and still runs, until the sound of his own footsteps without accompaniment frightens him, and brings him to a standstill before comment has been brought to bear upon him.

Another dingily respectable street, apparently bereft of life. The London Sunday street is, as a rule, dead. Just now this absence of things coming and going is a relief to the man. He stops short and looks back over his shoulder. Already ·the detestable idea of being followed has become part of him. Furtively he wipes his brow, and this lifting of his arm sends a sharp thrill of pain through his body. He pauses, looks mechanically upon the arm that pains him, and as memory grows riper a sweat of terror replaces that other damp he has just brushed from his forehead. *He must have used force with that old man!*

Such a frail old man! He remembers him now. Bent, feeble, yet vigilant. Vigilant, smiling and full of life; hard to kill. Good heavens! to kill!—yes, with that look of vitality in the quick eyes one *could* not kill him unless one resorted to extreme violence, unless, indeed, one *meant* to be—a—murderer!

Oh! . . . .

But what is the matter with this arm? a wrench, no doubt, in getting through the crowd—in that conflict with the policeman, say. It certainly had nothing to do with the old man. Oh—*damn* that old man! Why should he have come in his way!

He stands, a little dazed, yet sufficiently alive to consequences to make it clear to him that he must pretend to see something. A sweet shop, with shutters half up, does his purpose, and here he pauses, studying with unseeing eyes the dirty lemon drops and attenuated sugar-sticks, and generally consumptive lollipops that adorn the melancholy windows. As he thus stands he mechanically rubs his hand down the arm that hurts him, and presently becomes conscious that his fingers are moist. Mechanically, too, he looks at them.

Oh, kind, forgiving God! Not blood! not *blood.* He had been unkind, cowardly, cruel, but——. A horrible damp bedews his brow. *This* blood must have come from that old man. But from where—his head perchance. There had been no sign of blood upon him, save that small sickening drop that fell from his nostril downwards.

Well, what of it! He pushes the stained hand out of sight, and rubs it in a shuddering, secret fashion against his coat. The simplest thing in the world will bring blood sometimes. He had not seriously hurt that old man—only stunned him; it was for self-preservation, and doubtless even by this time the old fellow was on his feet again, and organizing a search party to arrest him. He laughs aloud as he thinks of this. Oh, yes, he will forgive him that search party—that natural desire for revenge. He will forgive him anything, if only——. A thick, painful sob chokes him.

*   *   *   *   *

It is next morning, the 16th of July. Through the half-closed windows the sun is shining into a library, an exquisitely-appointed room, very different to that small, scantily-furnished apartment where an old man had lain prone; upon one of the tables a daily paper is spread wide, and bending over it is a human creature, from whose mental misery and despair let us all pray to be delivered.

One paragraph has riveted his attention. As he reads and re-reads it, his every hope in life lies dead—slain, as surely as that old man was.

"Terrible Tragedy!" The letters dance before his eyes, then grow into a sullen red colour, then fade, then change back again to a large and vivid black. There is no escaping them.

Yet, suggestive as they are of cruel harm done to some man or woman, they would have had no weight with the man now staring at them with dull, hopeless eyes, but for certain other words lying below them. These last, indeed, had been the first to catch his eye. A sleepless night, an unacknowledged dread, had driven him downstairs early—had compelled him, though already he feared comment, to demand the morning papers before the hour usual for the butler to deliver them. And when they were once within his hands, as they are here now, tearing open the *Times*, he scanned its columns with an awful tightening at his heart—"10, *Sandiford Street*."

Now that he really knows, he feels as if he

had known it for a long, long time.   A century it might be!   *Could* it be only yesterday?

"Oh, merciful Lord! to Whom life belongs, Who can give and take it—*must* this thing be!   Oh, that a miracle might take place! Create one, Lord; and let that old man arise and walk the earth, as he walked it only a few short hours ago."

This man, his slayer, praying now as he had never prayed before, stops short here, and flings up his arms heavenwards, as if sudden conviction of the futility of it all has struck with the sharpness of a keen strong blade into his heart.

It is too late.   The voice of Heaven has spoken; there is no appeal.   Henceforth he is accursed.

Again, as though compelled to it, he reads the fatal words beneath him, though were he to live a thousand years he could not forget them, so burned into his brain they are. "This last tragedy took place very close to the scene of the shocking murder on Saturday night, at that famous, or rather infamous, gambling hell in —— Street."

He beats his hand fiercely on the paper
here, and his horrified eyes grow bright with
a sort of rage, that cries aloud upon his folly,
In seeking to escape the world's censure on a
minor fault, he had fallen into an abyss from
which no man can pluck him.

"An old gentleman, a Mr. Darling, quiet,
respectable, and much thought of by his
neighbours—so thoroughly inoffensive in all
his ways that a motive for the murder is
impossible to find. The case is rendered
even more difficult by the fact that a desire
to rob had evidently nothing to do with it—
the murdered man's watch, chain and seals
being found upon his body, and some loose
coins in his pockets. It appears the servant
was out, and had left the hall door wide open
whilst she went on her errand. The murderer
must have entered by it, and finding the old
man alone, perpetrated his dastardly crime.
It is remarkable that two such fearful as-
sassinations should have been committed
within a few hours of each other, and points
to the clear idea that one crime suggests
another, and that the thirst for blood, like

a disease, is catching. The police have made every inquiry, but as yet there is no clue to the murderer."

"No clue to the murderer!" Through all his despair his eyes cling to those last words. It is characteristic of the man that, in spite of the real agony he is enduring, no thought of voluntarily surrendering himself to justice finds room. That dread of public opinion—that shrinking from public censure—that has been part of his life ever since he was cognizant of anything, is strong as ever within him now, and in the very centre of his *dis*comfort he finds comfort in the thought that no possible opening for discovery lies anywhere. He had gone in and out of that house unobserved. His conscience alone had accompanied him as he entered and left it—a most sorry companion too, and one not to be silenced. Yet he is safe. In the very depth of his remorse and misery he sees that.

END OF PROLOGUE.

CHAPTER I.

" DEAREST MARIAN,

       " You know I hate writing letters unless I have something to put in them, but now I *have* something, so I sit down to scribble to you. The fact is, I must tell it to somebody or die. *Such* an adventure! When one thinks of the beautiful monotony in which we always live, one must acknowledge that anything so out of the common as befell us yesterday is to be regarded as a pure godsend. Well, introductions over, facts lie before you. You know of course that big house on the top of Maiden Hill that has been untenanted for so long, don't you?—and that of late the owner of it has threatened to put in an appearance and destroy the pleasure of a great many of us who loved to roam his woods at will? Well, he has come, and the way we found it out was—*murderous!*

"Still believing the pretty woods ownerless, the colonel and I set out for our usual midday walk through them, the dear old man declaring he would like to take a last bit of good out of them. You will understand that with the advent of a master at The Grange our wanderings through the woods would be at an end. That would be inevitable.

"Pushing my arm through his, therefore, I went afield, thinking of nothing more out of the everyday run of things than that perhaps we might meet an early dog-rose, or a late primrose, or a rabbit, or——

"I pause here to make the rabbit famous, because he did come, and in coming nearly blew us into bits. Bad little, *good* little rabbit! He *didn't* kill us, you see, and he has given us what would seem a very interesting acquaintance.

"Well, here is the rabbit rushing out of the copse on our left, and—piff—bang—off goes something, and here now is the poor bunny lying dead at our feet. Could tragedy farther go?

"It could, I can tell you, for if that shot

that slew him had been just a trifle more to
the right I don't think I should have been
able to scrawl this letter to you now. You
see I was walking just a *little* in advance of
the colonel, and it would have caught *me*. It
was a chance! Right across our noses went
the shot. You know the colonel's way when
angry; well, he was fairly started now. He
picked up the rabbit without a glance to left
or right.

" ' We may as well carry home our bag-
gage,' said he, speaking as cool as you please,
to conceal the fright he had got, for it *was* a
shock, I can tell you; and I myself was ' all
of a thrimble,' as old Betty would say.

" At this instant—(quite the *right* instant,
now, isn't it? I always will say, he *couldn't*
have staged it better)—a man came through
the bushes into the foreground—white as
death. It *wasn't* chalk; it was nature. His
gun was in his hand. Plainly, *the culprit!*

" ' Oh, you are safe—you are not hurt?'
cried he, as though the words were shot out
of his mouth as sharply as that last discharge
out of his gun.

" And here the colonel grew tremendous.

" ' Good heavens, sir!' roared he; 'what do you mean by firing upon the passers-by?'

" ' You are uninjured?' said the scapegrace, in a breathless way. It was all the apology offered so far.

" ' No thanks to *you*,' roared the dear colonel once again. ' One would think the taking of human life was a mere pastime to you. Why you'll probably turn out a murderer, sir, if you persist in your present ways. Call *that* sport!'

" It was really too bad of the colonel; the poor man turned a lively green; you could hardly imagine anything more horribly crushed than he appeared. Flat all through. I felt dreadfully sorry for him, because of course he hadn't meant it. If he had been a real murderer, he could hardly have looked more conscience-stricken—there came a look into his eyes that quite frightened me. I nudged the colonel, who was beginning a second tirade, and at that ungentle reminder he consented to draw breath a bit.

" ' I beg your pardon,' said the new-comer

—his voice was quite a mumble, you never saw a man so frightened. 'I can hardly hope for forgiveness. When I saw you the fraction of a second after my gun was discharged I thought——.' He paused here, and I turned my glance more fully on him. And indeed as I looked I thought to myself that in all probability we should have to carry home not only bunny but his slayer. I tugged at the colonel's arm to make *him* look as well, and gave him to understand in a very clever whisper that if he continued to abuse this poor man any longer *he* would be a murderer, but he was too far gone to be led into any reasonable path.

"'So you ought, sir, so you ought,' said he unrelentingly, and with terrible severity, though he certainly didn't know what the stranger had meant, as the poor man had not finished his sentence. 'Why, your confounded gun went off within an inch of my nose.'

"'And no mean target too!' whispered I into his ear, which set him off at once. You know the colonel's darling nose—what a Wellingtonian it is; and how prone he is to give way to mirth at the most untimely seasons. He now began to snigger.

" ' I *can't* explain how sorry I am,' said ' *the man.*' (He *must* be put in like this if one is to understand him, because a thing without a name is a puzzlement to the most abstruse.) ' It is no compensation, I know, but when I had fired I thought I should have fainted.'

" The colonel, who was still sniggering at my inane remark, failing to catch fire at this last apology, I took courage in both hands (they are small, if sunburnt, if you will re- member), and glancing behind his back at the culprit I gave him a grimace, meant as encouragement. Whoever he was, however guilty—and he certainly did look like a poacher in those legging—in all conscience he had now been scolded enough.

" ' You needn't go *on* fainting,' said I, seeing that he was still very low down in the world. ' We are all here—none of us dead ; not so much as a *hair* of us blown into space ! '

" And here I confess I gave way to laughter of the convulsed noiseless sort. It wouldn't have done to rouse the colonel. 'The man' looked back at me. It was as though I had given him a reprieve. He regarded me with a gratitude that was certainly far beyond my deserts.

"The colonel by this time having had his snigger out, now felt better towards man and beast.

"'Tell you what, sir,' said he, 'you gave me a shock that is hard to forgive. My niece here,' indicating me, 'would have been a loss impossible to replace.'

"I thought this very handsome of the colonel, but refrained from the expected confusion. I sustained myself as though I really did believe the sun would stand still at my demise.

"'I can well believe that,' said the unknown, with *so much* emphasis that I understood at once that in an ordinary tale it would be acknowledged that he had fallen in love with me. I felt the plot thickening. To be the ideal of an out-and-out poacher is, I suppose, quite as much as even the modern maid can aspire to. I knew I ought to be grateful, so I tried to look it. But, unfortunately, I could only look it at the colonel. Really, one can't be ready all in a moment to look sweet things at a poacher.

"'However,' went on the colonel magnanimously, 'I can afford to forgive you, as you won't be able to do it again. The owner of these woods is expected here shortly, and I suppose he will see that his—er—people—er —guests can handle a gun.'

"Evidently my uncle was uncertain as to whether the man with the gun was a servant or a guest. As for me I had no doubt he was a poacher; but I thought if I told the colonel so he might come to loggerheads with him, and a real murder might be perpetrated. As the colonel spoke the man looked down. I was right, then. He was abashed.

"'*I* am the owner,' said he in a low tone.

"Well, what do you expect happened then? We didn't go through the ground, anyway. I don't know what the colonel did—I never shall know—because I burst into an idiotic peal of laughter that *ought* to have made the welkin ring if it didn't. It was *too* funny.

When I recovered, uncle was looking a little
stiff, but was letting his hand be grasped by
the embryo murderer, which showed signs of
grace in both, surely. When one thought of
all the colonel had said, and his allusion to
the fact that the owner of the woods would
be sure to dismiss the owner of them, I confess it seemed to me too good to be true.
Such a little comedy! We parted from him,
I scarcely know how, and returned to our
home.

" 'Perhaps I ought to have asked him to
dinner,' said the colonel, hesitating on the last
step.

" 'Perhaps you oughtn't,' said I, with fine
scorn.

" 'But so inhospitable,' muttered the colonel.

" 'We're not in Ireland now,' said I; 'so
that though you *have* insulted a man, you
need not ask him to dinner.' At this the
colonel turned blue.

" ' D'ye *think* I insulted him?' said he.

" You as good as told him he was a duffer
with a gun, at all events,' said I.

" 'Well, so he was—so he was!' cried my

darling colonel, with so fresh and so hearty a
contempt once more, that even though we
were now upon the high road I turned and
hugged him.

"Well, that is all. But it *was* an adven-
ture, wasn't it? Certainly our first meeting
with Mr. Crawford, the new man—the next-
door neighbour—was full of life.

"I suppose you want to know something of
the 'deserted village' (it is always deserted
when *you* go away). 'Stands Scotland where
it did?' you would say. (Fenton-by-Sea
wouldn't scan, or I'd have put it in). It
does anyway; there has not been the slightest
change since you left us, six months ago.
The usual visiting is kept up; no two families
have fallen apart, each from each; the inter-
necine warfare between Lady Stamer and Mrs.
Vaudrey has been faithfully kept up; last
week indeed it raged. When I say that the
combatants came, not to blows but to letters,
you will understand that the affair was serious
indeed. And all about the clothing-club, so
far as I can gather. Isn't it silly? Mrs.
Vaudrey came to auntie, and told her all

about it ; *such* a tale ! It took two hours and
a half, and the colonel swearing all the time
in the back room, because the early dinner
was *on* and she—Mrs. Vaudrey—wouldn't be
off. Good heavens! Who creates such
women as *her*?

"And yet I'd rather have her than that
horrid Lady Stamer.

"Well, she kept on hammering the whole
quarrel into poor auntie's head, who you
know is incapable of understanding anything
unamiable.

"'Lady Stamer didn't know herself,' was
one of the remarks that ran all through the
long recital of her wrongs. I must tell you I
was present all through the interview, because
I knew poor auntie would have died if she
had been left alone—and what a grief to the
colonel and all of us!

"'Lady Stamer was mistaken if she thought
she could ride rough shod over the county;'
this was an echo to the first start. 'She,
Lady Stamer, might be a baronet's wife, but
SHE (double dashed), Mrs. Vaudrey, was a
baron's daughter, and entitled to an Hon.

before her name.' And so on, *ad nauseam*. Isn't it queer? And yet you know I can't help sympathizing with Mrs. Vaudrey, just because I can't bear Lady Stamer! *That's* queer too!

"The latter is in an awful mood just now, though the beloved son, Sir Bertram, is at home. Perhaps his charms cannot kill the *ennui* that always ensues on the advent of the unbeloved one. Yes—Eaton Stamer is at home too.

"And I wish *you* were. Hurry back, like the best of girls that you are. I miss you very much, though indeed a good part of my time is taken up training a little new pony that the colonel has given to Jimmy. How he *does* love that eldest boy of his! How he loves all the world!

"Ever your loving

"EVELYN D'ARCY."

CHAPTER II.

LAST night was wet; to-day is lovely. In the darkness, when all had slept, the rushing beating rain had descended with eager joy upon the unresisting land, and deluged it. It is still early in the summer. We are not, as yet at all events, half way through it; June is still young—a very babe.

A perfect torrent of sunshine is falling on the old house, smothered in ivy as it is. The leaves glisten and sparkle and really quite preen themselves beneath its rays. It is evident that they like such ardent courting.

That it is an old house, and loved, though ill-kept because of want of means to keep it better, may be read by all who run. The sashes of the many windows are sadly in want of painting; the walls would be the better of a thorough washing—wherever the ivy, that in kindly friendship has covered their de-

ficiencies, is not, they show themselves unmis-
takably dingy.

But the sunshine riots over all. It gilds
the lovely and the unlovely alike. It covers
this English home of this Irish Colonel D'Arcy
with as much glory as it gives to the palatial
residence, little used, of the Duchess of Carminster, that stands on a high hill to the left
of Firgrove, the name by which the modest
mansion of the D'Arcys goes. It had been
so called when the colonel took it, and he left
it so, though to tell the truth there isn't a fir-
tree within a mile of it. There are others as
good, perhaps, or better—beeches and oaks and
elms, but of even a paltry spruce it is innocent.

Down below, in the field at the eastern end
of the house, a scene is being enacted that is
rather out of place when one thinks of the
terrible heat of the day. It is so warm,
indeed, that people of mature years creep
into darkened rooms, and seek couches, and
betake themselves to the last novel, and
generally efface themselves until the hour
comes when afternoon tea is here and the
intrusive sun is not.

But to the very young, heat and cold are alike. They feel them, but fail to classify them; they decline to abate one moment's ardour because of them. And thus it comes to pass that Evelyn D'Arcy, in a gown of the very oldest, and with half her lovely hair unbound and with the other half coiled on the top of her shapely head in orthodox fashion, is to be seen pursuing a rough little pony— youthful as herself, if one arranges the different terms of life honestly—round and round a grass field under the rays of a tropical sun.

In this delightful occupation she is helped by a boy cousin some four years younger than herself. Jimmy D'Arcy is indeed only thirteen, but an excellent assistant for all that. Excellent as he is, however, the pony is one too many for him; just as the little lad has cleverly driven him into a corner, with many a shout, and much uplifting of the arms, and threats and coaxings mixed, the merry little brute turns swiftly round, kicks up his unshod heels, and is off to the opposite side of the field before you could say Jack Robinson.

"Oh, Jimmy, what a *fool* you are!" cries

Miss D'Arcy, rushing up breathless. "Why, there he was, under your very nose, and you let him go. You'll never get such an opportunity again. His mane was in your fingers. Oh! what a useless, *useless* creature is a boy!"

"Well, I don't want to be kicked if *you* do," says Jimmy candidly. "Did you watch his hind legs—did you ever see anything like them? Round and round they went like a windmill. I don't believe any pony kicks like him. No one could be up with him. Now, Evelyn," excitedly, "here he is again. Now, be careful—I——"

But words are lost on Evelyn. She is once more off in wild pursuit of the refractory pony. Away goes the pony, its uncombed mane flying in the wind; away goes she, her pretty soft love-locks, that should lie decorously above her forehead, flying wildly too. This is the only analogy between them, as the pony is a stout sturdy little animal, with a thick neck, a restless eye, and at this present moment a plain determination to defy the world.

Evelyn looks as if she could defy the world too, in right of her beauty. She is a little thing, slender, dark-eyed, clear-skinned, with nut-brown hair, and lips as red as roses. A beautiful child—but as yet a child only, although she is quite seventeen. Her hair falls in light natural waves above her white brow. Her hands and feet are models; even the rough shoes that cover the latter cannot hide this fact.

Her eyes are peculiar—very large, and at times earnest—but deep and restless and sometimes mischievous. Brilliant eyes, that can be dreamy, angry, merry, gentle as the moment demands. There is something about her that suggests the idea of perpetual motion. An untamable creature hard to catch—as hard to catch as the wild little untrained thing she is now pursuing with a foot as light as Atalanta's.

Jimmy follows, his heart in his mouth. He is a well-built lad and a handsome too, as all the D'Arcys are, with eyes afire with eager desire for conquest, and a mouth sweet and happy.

"Now, Evelyn—*now!*" he roars, racing up, but Evelyn has seen her opportunity as well as he. Rushing in upon the pony, she seizes his mane, and with an angry word or two to him—who knows her well—she reduces him to a certain propriety of demeanour. He consents, at all events, to stand still whilst meditating a fresh act of insubordination.

"Oh, you have him," cried Jimmy radiant, coming up and helping to slip a bridle over the captive's head. "*Isn't* he a beauty! And to think he is all my own. Say, Evelyn, isn't it good of father to give him to me?"

"You're in luck, certainly," says Evelyn, who is stroking the pony's nose, and whispering little loving words to it, that are received by the pony with a calm contempt.

"It's the best luck I ever had. I've always so longed for a pony, and now I have it. And father might have sold him, you know, and got money for him——"

"And money is rather an unknown quantity here."

"Yes. That's it. Perhaps," says the boy,

with a rather wistful look, " I oughtn't to take him."

" Oh, yes, you must. The colonel means you to have him. He's been arranging about it ever since last January. It is your birthday gift. It would trouble him now if you said anything."

" Well, I won't!" plainly relieved. " But he *is* good, anyway."

" The colonel's an angel," says Miss D'Arcy with calm conviction. "There isn't any one like him alive."

" Sometimes," says the boy, looking at her over the pony's shoulder. " Don't you wish he was *your* father ? "

Evelyn laughs.

" I don't see what difference it would make," says she. " If he were ten times my father I couldn't love him more, or he, me. And besides, do you know, Jim," growing suddenly grave, " I wouldn't give up the memory of my real old father for a good deal."

" Well, just so," says Jimmy vaguely.

" I wish we had a saddle," says Miss D'Arcy,

regarding the pony with a careful eye. " 1 could do without it, of course, but still a saddle is training."

" I'll run up to the stables for one."

" No. It is too far, and he might give me the slip again. I'll try him as he is. Here, hold his head ; keep your hand on his nose— *so.* And I'll make a jump for it when his head is turned the other way. Now, steady!"

In a second she has vaulted on to the pony's back, and with the quickness of practice has the reins well in hand.

" Let go," cries she sharply, and Jimmy, relaxing his hold on the reins, away flies the pony like a mad thing, Miss D'Arcy clinging to him like a limpet. Round and round the field they go, victory on neither side, until at last chance gives the pony the upper hand. Swerving against a post in the railings, he recoils heavily, flinging his rider to the ground.

" Great Heaven! She is hurt," cries a voice from the other side of the railings. The voice is followed by a face, white and disturbed, that rising from the drop into the field

beneath, where the mad struggle could be
seen from afar, now becomes level with the
scene of action. Driven by his anxiety, he
mounts the ha-ha as swiftly as a boy. He is
not so swift, however, that he cannot be outdone. A younger, slighter man, springing
over the wall upon his left, rushes towards
Evelyn, and——

CHAPTER III.

"I'M all right. What a fuss about nothing!" says she, springing nimbly to her feet, and speaking with a rather petulant air. No one likes to be commiserated on a fall from a horse, and this being a pony, the sympathy is even more objectionable. "Why, what did you think? That I was dead?"

"God forbid," says the young man, lightly enough, yet with something underneath that turns the careless rejoinder into a thanksgiving.

By this time the man who had so laboriously overcome the difficulties of the ha-ha, now comes into view, and resolves himself into Mr. Crawford.

"What! Two witnesses to my overthrow," cries the girl, a hot flush mounting to her brow. "Oh, this is too bad. But I do assure you, Mr. Crawford, that, as a rule, few horses can overcome me. By the by," with a rapid glance from one man to the other, " I suppose you are as yet strangers to each other. Let me introduce you. Mr. Crawford—Captain Eaton Stamer ; this is our new neighbour."

"Terribly new, I'm afraid," says Mr. Crawford with his slow smile, that moves as unwillingly as if it had been out of use and unoiled for many a year. As it stands, however, there is a certain fascination in it, born of its melancholy. Nevertheless, it fails to attract Eaton Stamer, who acknowledges the other's salute very coldly.

" There is something appalling about being the last new-comer," goes on Mr. Crawford, with that unwilling smile of his, that is now distinctly propitiatory. " One hardly knows where to tread. One knows nothing ; and one has got to find out all about one's neighbours without any help."

" And your neighbours have got to find out all about you," says Captain Stamer indifferently.

There's a second's—*just* a second's—pause, and then——

"True!" says Crawford slowly, with a gracious inclination of his head, as if in acknowledgment of the truth of the other man's idle remark.

"Well, I expect we'll find it out quick enough," says Evelyn gaily. "Nothing escapes *this* county; and if it did it would be snapped up by——"

She cuts herself off short and colours vividly, and gives an apologetic glance to Stamer.

"I forgive you," says he in a low tone and with a laugh, "though these allusions to my mother are of course painful."

At this Miss D'Arcy laughs a little too, and as Jimmy has now come up to them, pony in hand, a turn is given to the conversation.

"Take off the bridle, Jimmy; we shan't want it again now," says she with an ill-suppressed sigh of disappointment.

"And a very good thing too," says Stamer stoutly, deaf to her regret.

Mr. Crawford, however, is not so case-hardened.

"We are in your way," he says. "And

yet, is it safe for you to ride such an untrained little brute as that?"

"Why, a fall from *him* wouldn't hurt a
kitten," says Miss D'Arcy. "You should see
me sometimes when I've got a colt in hand.
Why——"

"I don't want to," says Mr. Crawford
quickly. So quickly, and with such evident
meaning in his tone, that Eaton Stamer turns
a sharp eye on him. Had *fear* been expressed
in it, or what?

Evelyn too has noticed the strangeness of
the tone and has laid her own constructions
on it. He thinks her unfeminine, wild, ungentle. A hot burning flush mounts to her
forehead; Stamer, looking at her by chance,
sees it.

"Miss D'Arcy rides beautifully. She is
quite fearless, and can manage most things,"
he says in a studied tone. "For myself, I
like a woman who can ride."

"Oh! Eaton," cries Miss D'Arcy, as if
startled out of herself by this bold declaration,
"why, only last week you told me——" she
stops quite suddenly here as if puzzled by a

4—2

glance he has cast at her. He laughs, more
for Mr. Crawford's edification than through
genuine mirth.

"Well, what did I tell you?" asks he;
and then quietly, "You have taken the
Grange, I hear, Mr. Crawford? Good house,
fine view. Best bit of cover in the neighbourhood."

"I think I shall like the place," says Crawford in his slow way, that seems to have
been acquired, rather than born with him.
"Though," with a glance at Miss D'Arcy,
who is now walking very demurely beside
them, "my first day here was hardly a
propitious one. I very nearly shot Miss
D'Arcy."

"*What?*" says Stamer.

"Yes." In a few words he tells the story.
"I came down here to-day, Miss D'Arcy, to
apologise to you and your father for my unpardonable carelessness."

"To my uncle," said Evelyn, correcting
him. "But it was no such great matter after
all. Nothing happened. We had not even
the good luck to get a grain. *Then* one might

have posed indeed as killed and wounded!
But as it was——"

"I could not sleep last night through thinking of it. It was such a mere chance. One
step more and—it might have been terrible,"
says Mr. Crawford with feeling.

"That word *might* applies to so many
things. Well, you haven't killed me, so be
happy. I shall never forget your face," says
she, giving way to uncheckable mirth. "It
was ghastly. Had my corpse been lying in
your path you could not have looked more
confounded." She turned her eyes to his.
"You would make a bad murderer," says she
gaily. "You would be found out at once—
your face would betray you."

His face now at all events is a study. She
has described it as being ghastly on their last
meeting, when his careless shot had been so
nearly fatal; but its hue was healthy then to
what it now is. After a moment he rallies,
his colour creeps slowly back into his face,
but his smile is still fixed and singularly unpleasant as he answers her.

"A good thing," he says. "Better be

found out at once, than live a life of secret horror."

"You speak with feeling," says Captain Stamer laughingly. "Had you a friend who 'made away' with anybody? That's the correct phrase, isn't it?"

"Oh! there's the colonel," cries Evelyn quickly. A figure on their right can now indeed be seen, making a vigorous but futile effort to hide himself within the shrubberies. "Colonel! *Colonel!* Don't go! We can all see you; and you look twice as lovely in that old coat as in your Sunday-go-to-meeting one. Come back. Here are only Eaton and Mr. Crawford."

The colonel, with a rather shame-faced smile and a coat very considerably the worse for wear, but a cherished old coat for all that, and an unspeakable comfort to its owner, veers round and advances on them.

He is a tall man in the prime of life still, though he has passed his fiftieth year, with a remarkably handsome face and a grand carriage, and in spite of his shabby surroundings, "gentleman" written all over him. His eyes are as bright as if he was only fifteen, and his mouth is the image of Jimmy's. It would occur to the intelligent observer that the colonel and Time will have a tussle before the latter gains the day. It is certain that the colonel will find a real difficulty in growing old.

"Glad to see you—glad to see you," says he, shaking hands first with Crawford and afterwards with Stamer. "Warm day! I thought I saw ladies in your train, and—er—old coat, don't you know. Meant to cut round by the shrubbery into the house and put on some fresh toggery, but Evelyn circumvented me ; she generally *does*, ha! ha! You'll excuse me, I hope," turning to Crawford ; "I was gardening, putting down fresh row of peas—rats ate the last row."

"I really do think, colonel, it is disgraceful in a man of your age to be so given over to vanity," says his niece, tucking her arm into his. "The fact is, that you think you look beautiful always, and yet you must pretend that you don't. So *false!* I left Jimmy with the pony. I hope they won't both come to grief."

" Not they," says the colonel, who is of that
happy sort who never see breakers ahead.
" Why, here he is. How's the pony, Jim ? "

" A darling ! " says Jimmy, which is hardly
an answer. " Oh ! dad, I do *love* you for
giving him to me. Say, Eaton, isn't he a
beauty ? "

The group has got divided now, and the
colonel with Mr. Crawford are walking on in
front.

" You must come in for a bit and have something," says the colonel. " It's an awful hot
day. Mrs. D'Arcy will be delighted to see
you. She—ha ! ha !—she has come to look upon
you by this time as Evelyn's preserver. As
you *didn't* shoot her, you see, you saved her
life." Here the colonel laughs again, a mellow
laugh that does one's heart good only to hear.

" I shall be very pleased to make Mrs.
D'Arcy's acquaintance," says Crawford. " She
is very good to take it in that way." He
pauses a moment and then goes on. " Your
niece—is English ? " he asks.

" Not she ! " says the colonel stoutly, knock-
ing the ash off his cigar in a rather offended

sort of way. " How could you think that? Not at all," more broadly ; " her mother was my sister, Irish to the backbone, and her father's mother was Irish too. She took from them all the blood she has. There isn't," with triumph, " an English ounce in her."

"Ah!" says Mr. Crawford, "yes; one should have known, of course." Her mother, D'Arcy's sister. But what was the father's name? The father's mother had been Irish too. Probably they were cousins all through. The Irish are fond of intermarrying. Of course D'Arcy was her name—they called her so.

CHAPTER IV.

By this time they have reached the house, and entering it by a hall-door that would be very much the better of a coat of paint, are shown by the colonel into a large and shady room upon their left.

It is about as curious a room as one could imagine, made up of all sorts of incongruities so far as the furniture is concerned, and yet it is a distinctly pretty room. From the girl's careless beauty and her open unconcern about her dress, which is so ancient as to be at its last gasp—from the evident shabbiness of the colonel, Crawford, at all events, had been prepared for a drawing-room untidy to the last degree.

Yet this room is charming in its own money-less fashion. The chairs, if so old as to be almost worthless, still belong to the class that are found only in good houses. The elderly curtains are nicely draped. Great care has been taken with the arrangement of the few small tables. There are no antimacassars and, above all things, flowers reign everywhere ; there is a very profusion of them, all exquisitely settled in their bowls. Through the lowered blinds a brilliant twilight seems to cover this strange old room that is a veritable surprise to Crawford, seeing it for the first time.

"What roses!" says he, bending over a delicate bunch near him. "And how well contrasted. Your work?" to Evelyn, who is standing beside him trying to make tidy her shapely head. She has both arms uplifted in order to do this and continues the occupation whilst smiling a consent to him.

"Yes, mine. I always arrange the flowers. But the roses belong to the colonel. Roses love the colonel. He has only to look at them and they bloom straightway. I always say no credit should be given him. Don't I, colonel?"

"I certainly shan't come to you for a character, my dear, when I want one," says the colonel, giving a refractory lock of hers a pull, whereon all her work is undone, and her pretty rippling hair falls once again in a shower upon her shoulders.

"Oh, *bother!*" says she with a gay little laugh. Crawford might have been the oldest friend in the world, for all she seems to care about him. She lacks *mauvaise honte*, indeed, to a rather dangerous degree, but there is still something new and therefore fascinating in her utter want of self-consciousness. The colonel laughs too, and at this moment the door opens and Mrs. D'Arcy comes in.

A small vivacious woman, with kindly eyes and a rather inconsequent manner. Not fair enough to be called fair, and not dark enough to be called dark. Nothing definite. With a good word for everybody, and a warm heart, and a tongue that runs like a rippling stream, and a great affection for her husband and the children, of whom Evelyn is always counted one. Her "eldest girl," as she calls her, with a loving glance and smile at her husband's niece when she is introducing her to any one new to them.

"Yes, Mr. Crawford, she is *quite* my own daughter. I have had her ever since she was seven, and indeed a blessing she has been to me. And how do you like the Grange? Always a little gloomy it has seemed to me, but certainly very handsome, and Evelyn and the colonel think the woods perfection. Well, so do I. But I don't walk much, you see; I haven't time; there are so many children, and children mean trouble."

"I have seen one—two of yours," says Crawford, with a kindly remembrance of her allusion to Evelyn as a child also. "Master Jimmy. A handsome boy."

"Yes, isn't he?" a faint flush rising to her face. "Just like the colonel. Same mouth and eyes. The others, I'm sorry to say, take after me. No—no—not a word of that sort. I'm past believing in compliments, and we all can see that to be like the colonel would be an advantage. Well, and so you like Fenton-by-Sea? A pretty little village, isn't it? but so much want always amongst the fishermen. Mr. Vaudrey, our rector, is always lamenting about it. But Jeremiah himself could hardly

be of any use to them sometimes, when the
season is bad."

"Yes, I've heard. It is terrible. Such
want, such losses as there must be. I,"
hurriedly, "hope to see Mr. Vaudrey soon,
and get him to let me help him with those
poor fisher folk of his, on whom I'm told his
heart is set."

"Ah, he will love you if you will help him
there. And it will be good of you," says Mrs.
D'Arcy simply, her eyes brightening. "The
colonel does what he can, but then there is no
money!" with a little expressive wave of the
small brown hands. "One always feels as if
fishermen were specially to be cared for.
Our Lord chose so many of them to be his
followers. And indeed they are brave fellows
always."

"To be brave is to be great," says Mr.
Crawford in a low tone. He is looking down,
and now he twines his fingers round each
other, as if caught by some unpleasant recollection.

"You don't know Mr. Vaudrey yet?"

"I know nobody, except you and yours. I

cannot fancy I shall go farther without faring worse. But Mr. Vaudrey will suit me. I have heard him very highly spoken of as charitable, humane, a good man. If I *can* help him, it will be a pleasure—a great one, a sole one."

He stops as if checking himself; quite suddenly, he looks tired, worn-out; there is a "giving-up" sort of expression about his whole face.

"Oh, if you encourage Mr. Vaudrey like *that*, you will have the parish on your shoulders," says Mrs. D'Arcy laughing. "He has no bowels of compassion for the rich, he gives all that to the poor. A *good* man? Yes, he is *that*. The best of men. You will like him certainly, or rather you will respect him. Some people," with an introspective look as if she is privately classifying the "some people," "sneer at him as an enthusiast; but *I* don't, and the colonel doesn't."

Apparently with her the colonel's opinion is final.

"The world wants enthusiasts," says Mr. Crawford. "They are the poor man's best friends. The common-sense people think too long. Whilst they study the subject the poor man dies. It is a sort of 'live, horse, till you get grass.' You know the old proverb. All the time the good man full of common sense is straining his eyes through his spectacles to read who should and who should not get the blankets and soup and coals, the poor man is dying from cold and hunger and misery. I speak warmly, because," with a smile, " I fear I am one of the terrible common-sense ones, myself."

" You speak kindly, at least," says Mrs. D'Arcy, her gentle face brightening.

" It is all talk—talk," says he with a quick frown. " If I would help the poor it is only —that I would help myself."

" But you are not poor—you have nothing in common with them," says she simply, rather puzzled, as indeed she well might be, by his strange manner. But the dropping out of the conventional, fashionable life that has been so hateful to him all these years into the calm monotony of the country and into the friendly carelessness of this rather unorthodox family has upset the usual reserve that has grown to be part of him.

"True," says he, recovering himself. "What I meant was, that everything, even apparently good motives—a desire to raise the condition of the poor for example, as we are on the subject—is all nothing but pure selfishness. Thus we would work out our own——" he pauses.

"Salvation," finishes Mrs. D'Arcy.

"Expiation," returns he in a low tone. He is very pale. He makes a movement as if to throw back his arms—to breathe afresh. "There is something in this air that is enervating, I think," he says with a sort of laugh that is unmirthful. "And I have bored you with my platitudes, of course. You will tell me not to come again."

"Oh, no," says Mrs. D'Arcy earnestly, who in truth has taken a fancy to him—who is indeed, perhaps, a little flattered in that he has given her so much of his society.

"Well, I have frightened the others at all events," says he, looking round.

The room is empty.

CHAPTER V

THE colonel, seeing his new guest so well entertained by his wife, had given a wink to Evelyn, and with Stamer had slipped through the low open window into the straggling garden.

"Your aunt's wonderful—*wonderful*," he says to Evelyn, when they are safely out of earshot. "She can tackle any one. That's the sort of wife to have. Don't you marry, Eaton," with his jolly loud laugh, "until you get some one who can do all the talking for you. Save you a world of trouble."

"Any woman would do for that purpose," says Captain Stamer. Whereon Miss D'Arcy with great reason turns upon him and rends him.

"I like that," cries she. "One would think *you* never talked at all, and that we were educated magpies! Why, look at you, colonel!

I *never* knew such a chatterbox as you are. All the world has heard of the man who talked the hind leg off an elephant, but only a very few know that *you* are that famous person. Go to! And as for Eaton, there isn't an old fishwoman between this and Fenton who can scold as well as he can."

"*I* scold?"

"Yes, yes, *yes*. I am a living witness. You scold me, morning, noon, and night."

"You! Do you think I'd *dare?* Colonel, you might give a companion in affliction the use of your arm. I feel as if I were going to give way."

"Not you," says Miss D'Arcy with a tilt of her lovely nose. "You wouldn't give way to a saint."

"Why should I? I'd hate a saint."

"At that rate you leave yourself outside the pale of affection," says she. "For you'd certainly hate the sinner."

"Well, you are not going to chide him for that, are you?" says the colonel.

"Better love a sinner than be indifferent to all things," says she, still scornful.

"Tell you what," says Stamer suddenly, "Crawford's a sinner."

"Eh!" says the colonel, as if startled by the other's tone.

"Oh! it's all nonsense, of course," says the younger man, laughing. "I know nothing about him. He may be immaculate for all I know. And probably he is too. But I can't bear those fellows who keep their eyes upon the ground, and speak as if every word they said was being weighed."

"And found wanting," says the colonel with another healthy roar. "Did y'ever meet so dull a dog? I couldn't get on with him, not I. Yet you saw how Mrs. D'Arcy managed him. He looks as if life had gone ill with him—as if he'd lost his sweetheart and his last penny; and yet for the latter, at all events, he is good, if accounts be true. Unsociable sort of a beggar he seemed to me, though no doubt there's good in him."

"I'm sure there is," says Evelyn quietly. "I can't think why you don't like him. I suppose in one thing you are right. I am sure he has been crossed in love. He looks just like that—so melancholy."

" Why don't you say, so interesting ?" says Stamer, with a quick look at her.

" What! you like him," cries the colonel. " Well, girls are odd. Now I thought you'd have turned up your nose at a worthless sort of fellow like that."

" He is *not* worthless," says Evelyn.

" No. He has got twenty thousand a year," says Stamer shortly. "Got a light, colonel ? "

" No—I don't know—yes, I have," says the colonel, bringing out a solitary vesuvian from some subterranean pocket. " And, by Jove, talking of Crawford reminds me that I ought to go in and get him a B. and S."

" He'll be too pious to drink it," says Stamer, who is evidently in a bad mood.

" Tell him *I* recommend it," says Miss D'Arcy, who is, it must be confessed, *tant soit peu coquette*, making a little *moue* at her uncle over her shoulder, " and he is sure to forget all his principles."

" I'll tell him," says the colonel airily, as he

moves towards the house, leaving the other two alone.

They have passed the drooping roses, now hastening to their death, and have come out upon a narrower walk, where branches of the strongly scented syringa brush them as they go by.

" You meant that," says Stamer with all the air of one who is defying her to deny it.

" Did I ? "

" Yes."

" Well, why shouldn't I mean it ? "

" Why should you not indeed. Still, let me tell you, it was rather a conceited speech for any girl to make about a man she had only seen twice."

" And here is a rude one to counterbalance it."

" I can't see that I've been rude," stiffly.

" Can't you," with growing displeasure. " Can you see that you have been absurd, then ? Not even *that* ? You *are* dull to-day."

" How am I dull ? "

" To imagine for a moment I meant such words as those. You know perfectly well

that I only said them because —to—well, because I was stupid too, I suppose, in my own
way. Not," with a little flash from her dark
eyes, " so bad a way as *yours*, however. Why,
as I tell you, I only saw him twice in my life
—yesterday and to-day—for a few minutes
each time! "

" It is true for all that," says Stamer in a
rather sudden fashion.

" What is ? "

" That you could turn him round your little
finger, if it so suited you."

" *Nonsense !* "

" He admires you already so much that——"

" I must really beg, Eaton, that you will
not talk to me like this."

" He does, for all that," says the young man
doggedly. " I could see it in every change
of his face. He could speak to nobody but
you."

" Not even to auntie ? " with a short and
unlovely laugh.

" Oh, as for that, he *should* be civil to her,
if he wishes to see you often. That was merely
kissing the nurse for the sake of the child."

" *Well!* " says Miss D'Arcy, coming to a standstill, and proceeding to examine her companion's face with quite an absorbing interest. "You *look* sane," says she; "but you can't be. Lunatics are very deceptive. Why, what can be the matter with you to-day? There is one thing, you used not to be— vulgar. Did you know you could be that?"

"Did you know you could lose your temper over a perfect stranger?"

"Over an old friend, rather. But if old friends prove unpleasant, why should one put up with them?"

"Well, I'm not going home yet, if that's what you mean," says Captain Stamer. "And I'm not going to quarrel with you either about a fellow like Crawford."

"I hope you won't quarrel with me about anybody," says she coldly. "And as to Mr. Crawford, where would the quarrel lie? Suppose, as you insinuate, that he *did* see imaginary charms in me, what is that to you, or any one?"

"What is it to *you?*"

"You refuse the question. The fact is, you

detest this perfect stranger who has dropped into our midst."

"I don't believe he is by any means a *perfect* stranger."

"That is very unjust. You know nothing to his disadvantage."

"Or to his advantage either."

"What on earth can he have done to you?" says Evelyn, with a rather exasperating insinuation.

"To *me*?" haughtily. "Nothing! I don't fancy him, certainly, but——"

"It is a paltry thing to dislike a man without a reason," interrupts she promptly.

"Well," says Stamer, "if you must have one, I don't like his face, his expression, his eyes, his mouth; there is something that might be termed generally, 'repression,' about him. He looks as if he might go off at any moment without a word of warning. He should be labelled 'Dangerous.'"

"'Glass! This side up with care,'" quotes she contemptuously. "Well, if *that* is all."

"It really is all, I'm afraid," with a regretful smile. It is plain that he would have found pleasure in bringing facts to bear on Mr. Crawford's implied unpleasantness if he could, and is quite frankly sorry that he can't. "You must admit, however, that his face is out of the common."

"A charm, surely. In a world where every one—who has not had the advantage of being blown up—has two eyes, a nose and a mouth, there is certainly a distinction in being able to look a little different from one's fellows."

"Not in his case, however. He'd be more agreeable if he were more like his fellows. Commoner, no doubt, but more human. Why," with a touch of irritability—"why can't he smile properly?"

"He *does* look sad, doesn't he?" says she eagerly; "that struck me too. Some grief, some *hidden* sorrow is troubling him. Perhaps——"

"Oh, perhaps, perhaps," interrupts her companion, with disgraceful rudeness. "If you are going to pity him, there's no more to be said. When a girl begins to pity a man, there's no stopping her. We all know where pity leads."

" Do you know where this path leads? " asks
she, with astonishing sweetness. But *he* is not
astonished by it. He understands it.

" If one were to climb over that wall in front
of us, it would probably lead one home," says
he, as if declining subterfuge. " But I hate
climbing. And, as I was saying, I think any
pity you may lay on Crawford will be a dead
loss. To my coarser vision there is nothing
sentimental about him. Nothing, except——"

" What? " sharply.

" I don't know," lamely.

" I wonder you aren't *ashamed* of yourself,"
says Miss D'Arcy, with deep contempt. " You
are trying as hard as you can to take away
that man's character, and all for what?
Through sheer idleness. You want to pre-
judice me against him."

" I do," gloomily.

" But why, *why?* " impatiently.

"I don't know. I don't like the fellow.
There's something queer about him."

" He's your Doctor Fell," says she.

" Well, perhaps so," says he, as if tired of
the argument.

Here, indeed, both the combatants, as if tired, lay down their arms for a season, and silently proclaim a truce. A brittle one; their tempers being still on edge, they tread softly as if afraid to venture beyond a certain limit.

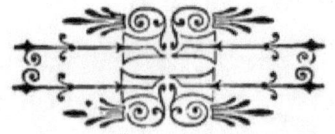

CHAPTER VI.

"Lovely day," says Captain Stamer, by way of proving the freshness of his geniality, with an exhaustive look around him. Alas! the day refuses to support his kindly judgment on it. Demon-like, it betrays him. The rain of last night, that this morning—nay, that five minutes ago—had seemed to be a thing so remote as to be placed in the category of injuries over and done with for ever, now with an angry rush flies up from the sea, and threatens to envelop them at any moment.

"Delicious!" says Miss D'Arcy, with a stern determination to agree with him on every point in spite of all obstacles. As she speaks a huge rain-drop falls into her left eye. "Pah!" says she, digging the knuckle of her little first finger into the insulted member.

"It is only a summer shower," says Stamer, glancing however with keenest suspicion upon

the lowering heavens above. The blue has
disappeared, the gilded clouds are gone ; there
is nothing left but greys, and such dull pig-
ments.

"Nothing more," says she valiantly, although the drops are pattering now so hard
about her feet that the gravel seems to rise
to meet them.

"Come in here. Come quickly!" cries
Stamer eagerly, forgetting his *rôle ;* and catching her by the arm he runs her into a dilapi-
dated summer-house hard by, that seems fit
to harbour only beetles, slugs, and such wild
beasts.

It is a little haven, however, for them, as,
however bad it is, it keeps out the heavy angry
rain that June sometimes as if in malice sends
down upon her admirers. Perhaps she is a
coquette this June of ours, that we all love,
and finds a mad delight in scattering abroad
and bringing to great grief the sincerest of her
admirers.

"Pouf! Who'd have thought it?" says
Evelyn, with a little light laugh, shaking the
dewy drops from her head and hands—her

charming head that is hatless, and crowned only by its own lovely curls.

"Who, indeed. It was an ideal day, two minutes ago. Are you sure no rain is coming through there? No? Come closer to me. This side seems the most waterproof."

"I'm all right," says Evelyn, refusing this inviting offer.

"I hear this tennis tournament is coming off next week."

"Yes, and I'm so sorry; I had so wished that Marian would be home for it."

"Well, she will be. My mother had a letter from her this morning, saying she is to be back on Friday next."

"No? *Really?*" turning an eager face to his. "Are you *sure?* Oh, I *am* glad! And she will play, of course. Now I can feel some pleasure in it."

"Have the players been drawn yet?"

"Oh, no! Nor handicapped either. I think your brother is to be one of the handi-cappers."

"Who has got up this affair?" asks Stamer, who has been away with his regiment and has only just now returned on a three months' leave.

"Mrs. Vaudrey."

"I wonder the rector stands such a burst of frivolity."

"Mr. Vaudrey is not so narrow as all that. He may devote his own life to the poor, but he does not expect every one else to do the same. He likes to see people amusing them-selves. He says tennis is a healthful amuse-ment."

"Ah! His own girls are growing up," says Stamer. "That's the way with all of them. I knew a parson once who thought dancing one of the cardinal sins. He preached steadily against it for fifteen years, yet the first thing he did when his eldest girl was thirteen was to engage a dancing mistress for her. They *must* marry off the girls, you see."

"I daresay, I daresay," says Miss D'Arcy vaguely, who has evidently not been listening. "Did you hear that the Duchess of Carminster is to be present at this tournament?"

"My dear girl! Have you not yet grasped the fact that I have been home a week, and

that the whole place is ringing with the news
that the duchess is coming *at last* to stay at
the Castle? I'm sick of the very name of the
duchess by this time."

"Well, I'm not," says Miss D'Arcy briskly.
"I'm longing to see her. Tell me what she is
like. One doesn't see a duchess every day, let
me tell you, and I'm not above wanting to see
a real live one before I die."

"Candid child! You'll be gratified, then,
for she's about as alive as they make 'em.
Honestly," says Captain Stamer, changing his
tone, "she's quite as nice a woman as ever
you met."

"You know her, then?"

"In a way. I've been staying with her now
and again at her place in Devonshire. She's a
widow, as, of course, you know."

"I don't. I never thought about her—
until now that she is coming. I suppose she
is a very grand person—very haughty, I
mean."

"She's not the orthodox duchess at all,"
says Stamer. "You know *they* are all born
old, *very* old. They are never young, but

this one is. They step into life full-grown, with high white hair and hook noses, and a *pince-nez*, and a supercilious glance that freezes everybody. And she isn't as haughty as she ought to be, she's—if one may be allowed the word where a duchess is concerned—rather *larky!* She likes people who make her laugh, and her guests are generally of the wits from the upper ten, generously filtered all through by a small stream of lesser folks that hail from Bohemia."

" And under which of those heads do you appear ? "

"Oh, as for me," says the young man frankly, "she only asks me when she has tableaux vivants or private theatricals on. I'm of use there, do you see ?" There isn't a spark of vanity about this speech.

"She's going to be at the tournament, anyway. She has promised Mrs. Vaudrey. She —Mrs. Vaudrey—is always darkly hinting at the fact that the duchess was once in love with her brother, Lord Sainton. I suppose we may take that with as many grains of salt as we like."

"Mrs. Vaudrey's a fool," says Stamer indifferently. "Duchesses don't grow on every bush, d'ye see, and so one makes a lot of them when one *does* find them. However, if she comes to the tournament it will give it an impetus. I wonder who you will be drawn with. If you are drawn with me," with a light laugh, "I pity the others."

"*Now* who is making a conceited speech?"

"Have you been thinking about that ever since? Well, you *are* a cross little thing."

"No, I'm not. Not a bit crosser than anybody else. It is you who have been out of temper all the morning, and why? If your mother has been as horrid to you as she is to everybody else," flushing hotly, "that is no reason why you should come here and be uncivil to me."

"How have I been uncivil?"

"In a thousand ways. If it *isn't* your mother then, what is it?"

She has turned to face him, her eyes angry. The truce plainly is at an end. Her little old cotton frock that clings so lovingly to her young, beautiful, *svelte* figure, catching in a

nail in the ancient summer-house, he stoops to
release it.

"Nothing," says he, looking up at her, a
trifle nervously, from his half-kneeling position.
"Only——"

"Only what?" imperiously.

"I wish you would give up training those
ponies and colts," says he, rising to his feet
and speaking with studied determination.

"Is that it?" says she, drawing her breath
rather quickly. "What a long time you have
been coming to it. And after all, why
should I?"

She has grown very pale, very defiant, and
the small slight fingers clasped together are
twitching nervously.

"Because it is abominable work for a child
like you."

"You think it unladylike; why not say it?"

"Well, I *do* say it," shortly.

"I shan't give it up for all that. What!"
blazing round at him suddenly. "Am I to
cease from helping the colonel, just because
you and your mother think me a hoyden?
Yes, yes, that's the word; I've heard it often

enough to remember it. I've been told that that is Lady Stamer's usual name for me."

" By whom? "

" Never mind. *That's* not the point."

" By Mrs. Vaudrey, of course. She would do anything to bring my mother into disfavour. But if she told you that *I* ever called you a hoyden or anything else disrespectful, she lied."

" It is as bad to think it as to say it."

" I have neither thought it nor said it."

" Oh! as for *that!* " says she with a shrug of her supple shoulders.

" What do you mean by that? " exclaims he, flinging his ill-kept temper to the winds. " That you don't believe me? Speak, Evelyn! "

" Now *don't* get into a passion," says Miss D'Arcy, with the most aggravating pretence at soothing him, rubbing him down, and reducing him to a proper state of calmness.

" Pshaw! " says he, turning away. The rain has worn itself out, and now once again the heavens are blue, and all over the west great fleecy banks of clouds are lying. Captain Stamer stepping into the brilliant light outside the summer-house, makes a step or two along the gravel path as if in mad haste to be gone, and then checks himself.

"I must say," says he, looking back at her with an angry expression, "you are about the most aggravating person I ever met in my life. I make a simple remark to you in the most friendly spirit about what *should* be for your good, and if I was your worst enemy, meaning an insult in every syllable, you could not have taken me more unpleasantly."

"How like your mother you are," says she, glancing at him over a very raised and unfriendly shoulder. "That's the way she speaks when she has been giving me one of her lectures. You needn't give me an additional dose. I know her."

"You don't know me, at all events," with a throb of passion.

"Quite well enough," nonchalantly. "And after all, it comes to this," cries she, "that I won't give up helping the colonel for all the old gossips and goody-goodies the parish contains. You call him my uncle; I call him not only my uncle but my father too. He has

given me so much love that I never can repay
him. He has hardly a penny, as you know,
except what he makes by his horses, and *no
one* can train them as I can." This with
conscious pride. "I have a *hand*, they tell
me; I can give them a mouth. He says himself that he wouldn't get half he does for the
young ones, but for me."

"He therefore sacrifices you." He must
indeed have been off his head when he ventured *this* remark.

"How *dare* you?" cries she passionately,
hot tears rushing to her eyes. "How *dare*
you so speak of the colonel? He—he——"
she pauses, as if unable to give voice to her
indignation, and two large pearly drops fall
down her cheeks. "You don't understand
him; you are incapable of it," she hurls at him
at length.

"I do—I do," puts in the young man contritely, rather frightened at the storm he has
raised.

"No, you don't. He would not sacrifice
any one. He is always sacrificing himself.
There is nobody like him, not one."

" He is the best fellow I know," says Stamer.
" But there is this. He doesn't see, perhaps—
he doesn't grasp the fact that a girl like you
should not be made a—a stable boy ! "

This is terrible. In his anxiety, his desire
to amend matters, he has waded into the
deepest depths.

" *Go home !* " says Miss D'Arcy, in a low
but terrible tone. " Was that your mother's
last comment upon me ? No ; not a word. I
won't listen. And indeed why should you
speak? you could never excel *that*."

" Forgive me, Evelyn," exclaims he anxiously,
shocked too late by his own words. " I could
not have spoken like that, but that I feel so
much. We are such old friends, and I—it
was the thought that *other* men might think
oddly of you, that drove me to such a rudeness."

" What other men ? " with a curl of her
lip.

" That Crawford, for example. He saw
you. He——"

" Mr. Crawford is a gentleman," interrupts
she curtly. " He therefore knows a lady

when he sees one. I am nót afraid of *his* verdict."

"After that, I may as well go indeed," says Stamer, deeply affronted; and with a slight bow to her he disappears amongst the bushes.

Miss D'Arcy, having upheld herself with much vigour in a most dignified position until the last faint sounds of his footsteps has ceased upon the air, now permits herself to fall out of line, and sinking upon the rickety old seat of the summer-house, that is the home of countless wriggling beasts, gives herself up to unbounded wrath.

He! *He* to dictate to her, to call her a stable-boy! Why, a tom-boy wouldn't have been half as bad. He was insulting, insolent, hateful! And if he thinks she is going to endure such impertinence as that, he—he—well —he *little knows*. And after all, what business is it of his if she rides colts and ponies from morning till night? Who is he that he should object to her pursuits? Is he her brother, or her cousin, or her—aunt? The word seems to drop in quite naturally.

Miss D'Arcy startles the earwigs by a sar-

donic laugh. A maiden aunt—an old maid,
that's what he *ought* to be ; with his perpetual
lectures and fault-findings. Really it is too
much of a good thing that he should give
himself such airs with her.

Say he is an old friend. The oldest friend
she has. Very well then. But even the
oldest friend has no right to exceed certain
limits ; and he has exceeded everything. He
has called her horrid names, and laid down
lines for her as though he were the arbiter of
her destiny. And *what* a name to call her!
Certainly there are times when Eaton gets
past enduring. And does he think she is
going to pass over this last crowning insult in
silence ? Not likely !

It will be many a long day before she will
speak to *him* again.

Feeling wonderfully relieved on coming to
this violent determination, she springs to her
feet and makes her way to the house, still
raging as she goes. She'll let him *see !* *She'll*
punish him !

CHAPTER VII.

THAT good old romp called Tennis, is always in high favour at Fenton-by-Sea. Not a man, woman or child there, independent of crutches, or out of the perambulator, but plays it all day long, from the middle of May, when they catch severe colds that last them well into the autumn, to the end of October, when they contract severe coughs that cling to them until the following spring.

Still " vive le jeu ! " What can anything matter so long as one is well enough to wield the gallant racket, and knock out his neighbour's eye with the saucy ball?

There was once a naughty man with a bad disposition, who used to punish his enemies in such wise. Just give him the smallest reason for offence, and he would challenge you to a game of tennis that day, or next week, or the following month, and having got you he would dexterously plant a ball in your right orb and make you see stars for an hour or so. He would then apologize profusely. It was safe, and it was sure, and no man could swear he had done it on purpose.

Tennis is a good game, no doubt. What *would* become of the country folk without it? But that modern misery, the tennis tournament, can hardly be regarded as an unmixed joy. So far as my experience goes, I think it leads to more " evil speaking, lying and slandering," to more " envy, hatred, malice and all uncharitableness," than any other form of amusement extant. Indeed, perhaps if we throw in the " battle, murder and sudden death," we shan't be altogether in the wrong. Every man's hand is against every man ; chivalry dies at once. And in the smaller country places where these unfortunate collisions annually take place, the almost inevitable result is, that at least two or three families cease to be on visiting terms, the junior branches of each being so heavily afflicted with ophthalmia that they fail to see each other even when brought face to face in private roads, in drawing-rooms, or at church.

It is not indeed until the near approach of the following Christmas, when church decorations give a good field for flirtation, that their eyesight is mercifully restored, and they see and know each other again, until—the next tournament.

To-day the first tournament of the season takes place at Fenton-by-Sea. From time immemorial all public games have been carried through at Parklands, the residence of Sir Bertram Stamer; a tall, silent, lazy-looking man of about thirty-five, who had been in the Guards, but at his father's death, five years ago, had sold out, more to please his mother than himself, and come down, presumably to reign over Parklands. This trouble, however, his mother very considerately took off his hands, ordering and regulating everything so perfectly, and with so evident a determination to be queen regnant, that Sir Bertram, who is easy-going to a fault, sank into his secondary place at once.

She is a large woman, eagle-eyed, hooked-

nosed—very unpleasant. Ambitious for her
sons, now that ambition for herself is at an
end ; devoted to her eldest born, careless of her
second son—beyond the fact that he must
marry well, to raise the prestige of the family.
To this end, she is not only eager, but indeed
determined to help him ; and for this purpose
has selected a near neighbour of hers, a girl
of large fortune and good family, as a suitable
wife for him. That anything, that *any one*
should dare to step in and spoil her plans
would seem to her arrogance almost impossible. And yet there are moments when she
doubts, and doubting hates the author of her
fears.

Every one had been quite sure it would be
a wet day, so naturally it is a fine one. Early
in the morning the courts had been rolled and
mown for the last time, the dying roses in the
gardens plucked off, the walks swept, everything put in severest order. Not only the
neighbourhood, but pretty nearly the whole
county has been invited, and already the terraces and pleasure grounds are filling with
smart folk in their very best attire, who have

come presumably to see their friends defeated
at tennis, in reality to see the Duchess of Carminster, who has promised to shed a radiance
over the joust.

All the women are looking very jubilant,
the men a little depressed; just a few of them,
who in their white flannels may reasonably be
supposed to be embryo conquerors in the
struggle at hand, are marching about dropping
a word here and there, and evidently in overflowing spirits. Of these is Mr. Blount, a
beardless young gentleman of any age from
eighteen to twenty-eight, a nephew of Lady
Stamer's, now staying at Parklands; as he is
pretty nearly always at Parklands, this last is
scarcely worth recording.

He is a remarkably ugly young man, middle-
sized, stout, without a single redeeming feature except his eyes, which, if small, are so
thoroughly alive to the ludicrous as to be
admirable.

"I say, Evelyn, here you are," cries he,
pouncing upon Miss D'Arcy as she comes
slowly towards him across the grass, the
colonel beside her. "How do, colonel?

Nice chilly day for a game of this sort, eh?"

"Apoplexy, apoplexy, that's what it *will* mean," says the colonel. "Thought I'd never get here. Every step was a misery. I'm getting old, sir, getting old."

"Bah! get along with you," says Mr. Blount, giving him a playful dig in the ribs. "I like to hear boys like you making fun of us old fogeys; bet you forty to one, colonel, you'll be a baby still when I'm a hoary-headed sinner. Seen Marian?" to Evelyn.

"Yes; just as we came here. She was with Lady Stamer."

"She was anxious to see you. I thought by her eye there was a scolding in store for you, and rather went out of my way to give you the warning wink; but unfortunately I took it into my head that you'd come by the short cut across the fields, and lo! and behold, you came by the orthodox avenue."

"You gave yourself a great deal of trouble for nothing," says Evelyn. "Neither she nor anybody else has seen fit to lecture me *as yet;*

not even Lady Stamer. However, I live in hope."

"You'll win to-day," says Mr. Blount with a nod.

"Oh, no. In the ladies' singles, do you mean?"

"Yes. I'll bet my bottom dollar on you."

"*Don't!*" says Miss D'Arcy, as if frightened. "Bartholomew"—such is his euphonious name —"Bartholomew," in a wheedling tone, "I wish you wouldn't speak like that. I wish you'd try to think I *wouldn't* win; it is so much luckier."

"Dear little superstitious Irish girl!" says Bartholomew, with a truly beautiful, if slightly hypocritical smile. "I'll accede to your wishes. I give up my honest opinion, and now declare to you that a worse wielder of the racket than your silly self I never saw; and that anything like your presumption in coming forward to try and win the golden apple of this year has, up to this, been unheard of. Will that do?"

"Mrs. Wylding-Weekes will win it," says she.

"She may—she may. She's rapid enough for that or anything. I do like that woman ; there's no pretence about *her*."

"I like her," says Miss D'Arcy, rather curtly.

"Well, so do I, my good child. Ain't I saying so. Give me candour before anything. Besides, she's tremendously amusing, which can't be said of every one. Heard of her last row with Weekes?"

"I don't want to," says Evelyn, Mrs. Wylding-Weekes' rows with her husband coming under the head of periodicals.

"It was Pouncefort of the 10th, this time," says Mr. Blount unabashed. "Weekes found him grovelling at her feet—'sprawling on the floor,' *he* called it—last Tuesday. There was a rather better display of fireworks than usual."

"I wonder you aren't ashamed of yourself, Bartholomew," says Evelyn indignantly.

"You wonder *she* isn't, you mean."

"I don't indeed. I don't care what people say. She may be a little bit of a flirt," regarding him anxiously, "but I don't believe

there is a scrap of harm in her. And she is
the kindest woman in the world."

"That's where it is," says Mr. Blount.
"She's quite too awfully kind, don't you
know. I entirely agree with you, my best of
girls."

"I can't bear you when you talk like that."

"Then I'll talk like *this*. Nice weather for
crops, isn't it? but perhaps a trifle too dry.
The coming harvest won't be as good as the
harvest all we old people remember gathering
two or three hundred years ago. Did you
know that Mrs. Dumpling's niece has married
the Marchmonts' groom? No? Oh, law! yes,
my dear; and they had——"

"Don't you think there is somebody else
you ought to show some attention to?" says
Miss D'Arcy severely, having regard to the
fact that he is her hostess's nephew; also
with a view to showing her displeasure.

"Not a soul. Isn't there anybody *you*
want to be kinder to than you are to me?
There is!" tragically, seeing a sudden unhappy change in her mobile face. "Who is
it? Let me know the worst."

" I suppose," says she reluctantly, " I ought to go and say how d'ye do to Lady Stamer. I haven't done it yet."

" It would be a step in the right direction certainly. Come, let's take it together. Like all doses, once down one feels the better for them—or at least one *should*. Shall I "—seeing with a glance that she shrinks from the small ordeal—" see you through it ? In these cases of assault and battery, it is always better to have a witness on *your* side."

" You may laugh," says Evelyn ruefully ; " but she is always so horrid to me that—— And what have I ever done to her ? " cries she petulantly.

" Ah ! that's just it," says Bartholomew, who knows exactly what she has done. " By Jove ! here *is* Lady Stamer. What a happy meeting ! My dear aunt, here is another young lady who is dying to tell you what a lovely day it is."

" How d'ye do ? " says Lady Stamer frigidly, giving Evelyn two reluctant fingers.

" How dy'e do ? " says Evelyn icily, refusing to press them.

On this ensues a deadly pause, that threatens to be eternal, but for Mr. Blount, who is nothing if not useful. To be ornamental has been put out of his power by malignant fate— or rather his mother, who in her time was the ugliest woman alive.

"Well, go on," says he, addressing Evelyn in a reproving tone. "You haven't said it yet. It *is* a fine day, isn't it?" reproachfully. "No need to tell a lie *this* time. Lady Stamer has only heard it on forty-eight occasions up to this, and is therefore as yet imperfect in it. Give her another lesson."

At this Miss D'Arcy, in spite of her nervousness, smiles — a rather wintry smile—and as here most opportunely a fresh-comer claims Lady Stamer's words and looks, she accepts her chance, and flies precipitately.

"I saw you safely through that, anyway, eh?" says Mr. Blount, who has flown with her, in a tone of much self-gratulation.

"You did. You did indeed," gratefully. "After that first awful 'how d'ye do?' I didn't know from Adam what to say next."

"I'm of the greatest use to all my friends,"

says Mr. Blount modestly. "I don't really see how they could get on without me. As I never quarrel with any one, I'm always at hand, d'ye see, to make up the incessant guerilla warfares that seem to be going on from morning until night amongst my acquaintances."

"Oh! I don't see that," says Miss D'Arcy. "You aren't the only peaceable person in the world, I suppose. You do give yourself airs, I must say. I'm not a quarrelsome person at all; not at all."

"Of course not. How could you think I alluded to you? Present company always excepted. My dear Evelyn, it would take a member of Parliament from your own land to come to loggerheads with you. I don't suppose you have a feud with any one living. I say, there's Eaton. Shall I call him? Hallo, Ea——"

"No, no," cries Miss D'Arcy, catching his arm. "*Don't!*" Then, as he turns a quizzical eye on her, "I mean—that is"—blushing a hot and lovely red—"I——"

"Not another word," entreats Mr. Blount

politely. "You are not on your oath, you know. You and he are not on speaking terms for the moment. I *quite* understand. And very natural too. Man as a whole is a melancholy failure. Woman, on the contrary, is a grand success. One can see then at a glance how impossible it is for the latter to put up with the follies—and *worse*—of the former. Eaton has—I can see at once—been playing the fool with a vengeance. As a member of his species I feel I should plead for forgiveness for him, but really I can't. I haven't the courage. I can see at once that the patience of woman must be at an end, and that man, the inconsequent, should be let run to ruin in his own way."

"*You'll* never run anywhere," says Miss D'Arcy wrathfully. "You won't even run *down*. You're a clock that will go for ever, without winding. I never knew any one who could talk so much nonsense as you in a given time."

"However small the line, perfection in it must count for something," says Mr. Blount mournfully. "I feel I am beneath your notice; but Eaton, happy fellow, apparently is not. You *can* show displeasure to him; you *can't* to me. This is indeed humiliation. But I rise from it to do you, the ungrateful one, a service."

"You needn't," says Miss D'Arcy, carrying out the character he has given her to perfection. "Lie as low as you like; I shan't be the one to rouse you."

"I am not to be deterred from my duty, Evelyn, by any such paltry asides. I understand you better than you do yourself. Eaton has been presumptuous. And too much of anything, we all know, is good for nothing. A little wholesome correction will be the saving of him, if indeed anything can redeem that savage—man."

"I assure you, Bartholomew, you have taken up quite an absurd impression. Eaton has not——"

"Now, my dear girl, don't waste your time. Fibbing to Bartholomew means always that. I run as I read, and I'm positive that Eaton has——Hah!" stopping short and staring at a turn in the avenue that can be seen through

the shrubberies where they are standing.
Not only his eyes but his ears are satisfied.
The heavy trampling sound of horses' feet
comes to them across the grass and trees.

"Now then!" says he, laying solemn hands
on Miss D'Arcy, and so turning her as to face
the house. "Hold up your chin; your face
a little more *this* way, miss, if you please,"
with a professional air. "Pull out your frock
—*so*. Now look at me and *smile*. Hah! that
will do. Now don't wink! For here's her
grace at last."

CHAPTER VIII.

HERE she is indeed, and in great feather apparently. There is a general sensation; an honest straining of necks to see her, on the part of half the community, a most dishonest attempt at indifference on the part of the other half.

Now she has reached the hall-door. Now she has descended from the carriage and is beaming blandly on everything and everybody.

Lady Stamer is hurrying across the lawn to receive her, raging furiously as she goes at the fact that Mrs. Vaudrey, her life-long enemy, is already hobnobbing with the duchess, becking and nodding at her with all the vigour (and it is a good deal) of which she is capable.

Mrs. Vaudrey indeed—to use her own expression uttered later on—has been careful to be *upon the spot* (wherever that may be) at the moment of the duchess's arrival, and has rushed forward to welcome her with as much effusion as though she were mistress of the ceremonies and Parklands to boot.

In fact for a full minute the duchess—who has not the Sainton family well in mind at the moment—and whose memory is not as good as her intentions—so considers her, and pours out upon her all sorts of civil nothings. It is only for a minute, however, and as providentially no names are named nothing comes of it.

"Ah! Here is Lady Stamer *at last*," says Mrs. Vaudrey, and her grace, with a little inward gasp and a strong desire for laughter, goes over it all again heroically.

"So glad! *So* charmed! What a quite too lovely place. And such a *delicious* day. Perfect queen's weather, isn't it? And this is Carminster," pulling forward her little duke, a small boy of about seven with a pretty rosy face and a stout pair of legs. His grace drags off his cap, after a hint from his mother, says "yes" and "no" in the right place, but in an absent minded fashion, with his eyes on the distant tents, where no doubt are the flesh-pots of Egypt, and generally permits himself to be made much of in a placid sort of way.

"Not half the manner of my Herbert," says Mrs. Vaudrey to herself with deep compla-cency, which indeed is the solemn truth; Master Vaudrey—aged nine—being one in a thousand so far as conversational talent goes.

And now the train sweeps on. It is coming this way. The duchess is flanked on one side by Lady Stamer and on the other by Mrs. Vaudrey, who refuses to be relegated to a lower position, and holds up her head valiantly as if to remind everybody of the Hon. that is tacked on to her name. In vain Lady Stamer frowns her down; Mrs. Vaudrey is in her most airy mood and is doing the amiable to the duchess, who takes her advances very pleasantly. It is all the same to the duchess. She has got to talk so much in such a length of time, and it isn't of the least consequence who is to be the recipient of her remarks. But to Lady Stamer all this is gall and worm-wood. Mrs. Vaudrey of all people—detestable woman—in a gown that might have come out of Noah's Ark, and a bonnet that will probably be the height of the fashion in a dozen years to come, but *not now*. And she had meant to have everything so entirely as it should be. A desire to fall on Mrs. Vaudrey and smite her hip and thigh is raging within her whilst she talks platitudes and looks mildly at her august guest.

Meanwhile the duchess, who is in exuberant spirits, and who affects a royal memory without having it, is walking about, telling everybody how delighted she is to see them again. As it is fourteen years since last she was at Fenton, this is remarkably good of her! Few of us are so constant in our friendships. It is perhaps a little unfortunate that some of those upon whom she presses this old friendship—whom she makes a point of specially remembering—should be people who never saw her until this afternoon.

However, this breaks no bones. Nobody is offended by it. It is always something to have shaken hands with a duchess.

She is an extremely big woman, young still,

with a florid complexion, large violet eyes, hair the colour of a tar-barrel, and no nose to speak of. The daughter of an earl and the wife of a dead duke, she has yet about as much the sacred touch of race about her as the orthodox milk-maid.

She looks as pleasant as you like, however, which covers a multitude of wrong features, and goes about now beaming, like the sun, on the just and the unjust alike. She is attended by a host of satellites besides Lady Stamer and Mrs. Vaudrey, people staying with her at the Castle, and chosen rather indiscriminately, to say the least of it.

The business of the day has commenced. The battle rages fiercely. The hot sun, regardless of the comfort of the players, is pouring down its rays upon the several courts in a strictly impartial fashion.

Evelyn, having come victoriously through one single, flings her racket to the colonel, who is absurdly proud of her success so far, and drops thankfully into a low seat near her.

"What a good-looking child!" says the duchess. "And can't she *play!* I really hope she'll win. So nice to be able to run about like that and defy old Sol. I should think the prize for the ladies' single is sure to be hers; I'm thinking of getting up some theatricals or tableaux at the Castle, and— does that little girl belong to this neighbourhood?"

" Well—not exactly," begins Lady Stamer in her chilliest drawl, but Mrs. Vaudrey interrupts.

" Oh, yes; quite near, close at hand," says she briskly. " And she is such a dear girl. Nice people altogether ; but poor, you know, poor."

" That's nothing," says the duchess, with great geniality. I daresay she has taken a good-natured glance at Mrs. Vaudrey's gown.

" Just so—just so," says that irrepressible person. " The colonel, her uncle, is delightful. They are Irish, you know, and——"

" Irish—how interesting ! I *knew* there was something queer about her," says her grace, with all the air of one who has just discovered a wild animal of an interesting

species. "Positively I must get an introduction."

Not yet, however; the final tie is being
now played, and Miss D'Arcy is once again *en
évidence*. She looks like a slim fairy flitting
here and there, taking her balls without
a mistake, and seemingly without exertion.
The heat that has made her opponent—a
daughter of a neighbouring squire—almost
apoplectic, has given her only an undue
pallor. It is a sharply-contested game, but
the sequel leaves Evelyn the winner of the
gold bracelet that the duchess has kindly
consented to give away.

Pale, tired, yet certainly and very naturally
filled with a sense of triumph, she makes her
way swiftly across the court, to a little corner
behind the rhododendrons, that is so out of
sight as to be unknown to the many. Eaton
Stamer, as she passes him, gives her a glance
of congratulation largely fraught with appeal,
but taking no notice of it she leaves him
behind her unforgiven, and finding her
coveted recess, throws herself upon the rustic
bench, and draws her breath in long sweet

gasps. Oh! what a struggle it has been. Her enemy was strong—but how sweet is victory!

She smiles to herself in a little exhausted way as she leans back against the seat. She is indeed almost too tired to show resentment when a tall, gaunt figure, coming up the path upon her right, stops before her.

CHAPTER IX

"It was folly to play like that on such a day," says Mr. Crawford almost vehemently, his usually subdued manner quite shaken. "You have over-exerted yourself."

"No, no," says she, smiling again. It is impossible to be angry with this melancholy, quiet man.

"You have!" says he with decision. "You are looking terribly white."

"Better than looking terribly red," says she, with a slight laugh that is suggestive of tears, so full of fatigue it sounds.

"You are thinking of your adversary," says he with a half-smile. "Poor girl! she was twice undone. But it was presumption on her part to dream of defeating you. However, we may let her go by. As you are storng, I am sure you are merciful."

"I assure you she was a worthy opponent,"

says Evelyn. "You need not think I won
easily. It was as much as I could do to
cry 'Victory!'"

"I can see that," says he. "You are very
tired; you must not stay here any longer in
the sun. Come"—holding out his hand to
her with an air of decision—"come with me
to one of those tents over there, and let me
give you some iced cup or—well, water, if
you prefer it."

Evelyn, rising mechanically, follows him.
That iced water had a tempting sound. It
somehow gives her pleasure, too, to be able
to refuse any knowledge of Eaton Stamer's
existence as once again she passes him, Mr.
Crawford by her side.

Inside the tent coolness reigns as well as
solitude. Evelyn, sinking thankfully on to
a seat, accepts with gratitude the iced water
that Mr. Crawford brings her. Even here
through the chinks of the awnings the hot
sun sends a ray every now and then, and
from afar off the music of the band, so
suggestive of movement, of activity, comes
to them. Still it is delicious here—the very

far-offness of the world outside giving it a
charm. Too tired to care to talk, Evelyn,
leaning back in her chair, gives herself up
a ready prisoner to indolence. Mr. Crawford
may talk to her if he likes, but she—she
cannot talk to any one.

And for five minutes or so Mr. Crawford
does talk, content to get a vague " yes " or
" no " for answer from the tired child, and
then, being of a nature that desires silence
for himself, he too drops out of the desultory
conversation, and except for the buzzing of
a dissipated blue-bottle that has got into a
wine-glass and is too intoxicated to get out
of it again, no sound can be heard.

Silence however is sometimes as irritating
as noise. Evelyn, waking up presently from
her delightful waking siesta, becomes conscious of the fact that neither she nor Mr.
Crawford have opened their lips for a considerable time. Is he angry with her ? Has
she been rude ? Thus startled into life, she
leans her elbow on the table, and turns an
apologetic glance on her companion.

It is thrown away. Mr. Crawford sees

neither her nor any one, save, perhaps, some being from his dead past. His thoughts are not here, at any rate, in this sweet, cool tent, with the sweetest of all companions by his side; they are straggling farther afield—or backward, who shall say? At all events, they are not happy thoughts.

His brows are knitted; his lips are compressed. One might easily imagine that the teeth beneath them are clenched. He is stooping forward with one hand bound within the other, and a pallor suggestive of a cruel strain upon the whole man covers his face.

Evelyn, gazing at him, feels a sudden sense of fear overcome her. Instinctively she shrinks backwards, and then, as if ashamed of herself, straightens herself again deliberately. Poor man! Some great, some unconquerable grief is his. And how silently, how nobly he bears it. Not a murmur, a whisper to any one. It must have been some woman who has made him sad like that— some woman whom he had loved long ago, and never forgotten. Perhaps she had loved some one else, and——

Animal magnetism here declares itself. Mr. Crawford feeling, without knowing it, the kindly commiseration of those lovely eyes, wakens hurriedly from his day-dream, and turning his head, finds her sympathetic gaze fixed earnestly upon him.

"Well?" says he, pulling himself together by an evident effort, and smiling interrogatively on her.

"Oh!" says she, flushing hotly; "I—it was nothing. I was only thinking that——"

"Yes?" questions he again, smiling still.

"That *you* were thinking," concludes she, very shyly, yet with a certain air of girlish audacity that is charming.

"I beg your pardon," says Mr. Crawford contritely; "you were right. I was thinking —thinking;" he pauses, and his face grows suddenly wooden; that past recollection that had been so full upon him just now returns again and strikes him dumb for the second.

"Well, so I said," returns she gently. Her voice breaks the unholy charm that binds him.

"I should beg your pardon," says he, growing all at once conventional. "I have

been neglectful of you. But it is a trick
I have fallen into, of brooding—brooding
always——" he checks himself, and sighs
profoundly. "It comes of much living
alone," he says presently.

"Then you should give up solitude. I
don't know where you have been before this,
but for the future you must give solitude a
wide berth," says she, in her kind little way.
"You will soon get to know us all, and then
you will give up that horrid brooding."

"I seem to know you now," says Mr
Crawford in a pleased yet troubled sort of
way.

"That is well; that is a beginning. You
have not met Marian yet, have you—Marian
Vandeleur? No? Ah, well, *she* will be of
use to you. Nothing morbid can live near
her. And you want a human tonic of some
sort, don't you?"

She is feeling honestly sorry for him, is
honestly anxious that means of some kind
should be found, and *at once*, to lift him out
of this slough of despond into which he has
fallen. To her tender heart it seems terrible

that he should be grieving always—always, for that lost and, presumably (for the sake of romance), false love of his.

And really, when one comes to think of it, there could have been no excuse for her. Mr. Crawford, even now, is a nice-looking person, if elderly; and twenty years ago might doubtless have been reckoned handsome. What did the girl mean?

And what constancy he has displayed! Quite something to marvel at in this present frivolous age. Poor man! So long ago, too, it must all have been, and yet he remembers it, apparently, as though it had been yesterday. What a heroic stability of purpose! He is still clinging to a romance that time has left far behind him.

"You should not think so much," says she, leaning towards him across the rustic table with what seems to him a divine compassion in her young face.

"Ah! give me a medicine for that!" says he quickly. "For thought—for the abolition of memory—that greatest curse of all!" He has spoken with evident impulsiveness, and now, as if shocked at his impulse, grows suddenly dumb.

This pretty child! this little half-grown scion of Mother Nature, with her big, interested eyes! Is she not a healing angel in herself, with her soft, gentle smile, her warm and parted lips?

"You have been unhappy?" says she very timidly, very tenderly, approaching his grief cautiously, as one might who is longing to lay a soothing finger on it, and yet scarcely daring the deed.

"Yes," says Mr. Crawford slowly, and no more. It is the baldest of replies to the most imaginative of questions.

"I can see it," says she, still full of eager desire to comfort him, and so far fascinated by his hidden, mysterious sorrow as to find it impossible to let it go by without her having a glance at it. "It"—lifting the friendliest of eyes to his—"it was a *great* trouble?"

"A great trouble," acquiesces he. And then, with a heavy breath that is almost a groan—"Such a trouble as few men, God grant, have got to endure."

He thrums absently upon the table as he says this; his face set, and with the brows drawn somewhat upward.

"Oh! I'm sorry," says she simply. Her eyes have filled with tears. With the gentlest meaning in the world, she holds out her hand to him across the table, the small pink palm uppermost.

Something either in her tone, her action, or his own memories so disturbs him here that he rises abruptly, stands irresolute for a moment as if battling with some hidden demon, after which, sinking back upon the seat once more, he grasps the little kindly hand and holds it closely, as though salvation lies within those fragile fingers. He trembles visibly. A mist floods his eyes and obscures her from him. Dear heaven! what pity! what kindness! But blind—unseeing. Would there be pity or kindness if she knew? Well, she shall never know!

"It must have been a great trouble to last *all these years!*" says Evelyn with heavy emphasis and increasing pity, unconsciously clinging to her secret belief that the trouble

relates to the days of his youth, and has had
a sweetheart for its centre.

"It will last for ever," returns he moodily.

"Oh, no! That is folly. You should con-
quer such a thought as that," says the girl,
shaking her head reprovingly. Nevertheless
she regards him with admiration. What
constancy! What faithfulness! All these
years, and still to feel so keenly. Ah! this is
real love!

"What caused it—your grief, I mean?"
questions she, very softly still, indeed almost
tremulously now; it is as though she is approaching sacred ground. Is not love always
sacred? And it is the most wonderful of all
things that he should have remembered all
these years. To her he is an old man, nearly
as old as the colonel—only a little younger
than the vicar.

At her words he has loosed her hand. Not
angrily, but slowly, slowly—reluctantly, but
surely, as if compelled to let her go.

"Was it," says she very tenderly—"was
it death?"

At this he starts to his feet, as though she

had stung him, and turns haggard, staring eyes on hers.

"Death—death!" says he hoarsely. "What should I have to do with death? Speak—explain!"

There is something so wild, so strange in his glance, that Evelyn, a little frightened, rises too.

"I only thought," explains she nervously, "that—that she might have died."

"She—*she!* Who?" he looks at her frowningly, like a man awakening from a dream—a bad dream. There is relief in his whole air. Miss D'Arcy grows very red and distinctly ashamed.

"I don't know *why* I thought it," says she in a low tone, lowering her eyes; "but," nervously, "I got it into my head somehow that—that you had loved some one once, and that she—had died!"

Mr. Crawford draws his tall, lean figure to its fullest height and makes a curious gesture, as if flinging something from him. Then he laughs.

"You fancied me a heartbroken lover,"

says he; " you imagined that I had once loved, and that my love had been taken from me, or had jilted me. Well, the latter fancy would have been likely enough. I am not a man whom women would care for; yet both your surmises (if you had the two) were wrong. In all my forty-five years I have never known what it is to love."

Evelyn stares at him as if he is indeed something well worth studying. Never to have been in love! Not even once! It sounds incredible. A devout believer in Dan Cupid, though as yet she has not succumbed to his bow and arrow, Miss D'Arcy regards with curiosity the man who has during a lifetime successfully defied him. A little contempt mingles with her astonishment. And another thing—forty-five! Is he telling the *exact* truth, or is he stretching it a little bit? Surely he is more than that. Quite an old man, with hair as grey as——

" Do you mean to say you have never been in love?" says she, looking at him with large, distinctly disapproving eyes. " One ought to be in love *some* time during one's life."

Mr. Crawford turns, the word "never" on his lips. His eyes meet hers. The lovely childish yet earnest face, the calm lips, the expectant gaze, all are before him, and as they grow upon him the word dies upon his mouth. It is as a flash, a stroke, a revelation, an instant's work; yet none the less, sure. The word that a moment ago would have seemed to him the truth, would now be certainly a lie.

Miss D'Arcy, who is watching him, too, laughs gaily. That undercurrent of feeling that has rendered him dumb is unknown to her.

"Ah! You shrink from the answer," says she. "And quite right too. I should not have put the question."

"Perhaps not," says he. "And yet, believe me, in all my life before I came to Fenton, I never loved—I never cared for one woman beyond another. Many women I have liked —not one have I given my heart to. So far I was blessed." There is melancholy in the closing sentence.

"Tut!" says she, as if disappointed. "Then

see how you have deceived me! Here have I been wasting, oh! any amount of sympathy on you, and after all, as it proves, for nothing. Do you think I shall readily forgive that?"

"I have fallen in your estimation," says Mr. Crawford. "I feel that. But would you have had me tell you anything less or more than the truth? I am not a happy man, as you may see. What should such as I have to do with a sweetheart?"

"Heretic!" says she with a pretty playfulness. "Don't you know that a sweetheart is the sovereign cure for all sorts of doleful dumps? Come, amongst the many beauties here to-day, surely I can find you a medicine for your fancied sorrows."

She has recovered all her wonted spirits. She is standing before him, smiling, beckoning him towards the opening of the tent.

"Why should I stir?" says he suddenly, following her fanciful mood, yet with deep meaning in his tone. "Can I not find my heart's ease *here?*"

He laughs nervously as if at his own temerity, and she laughs gaily in concert with him. It is a pretty joke, no more. She moves towards the open door, he following her, and here she comes face to face with Eaton Stamer.

CHAPTER X.

Miss D'Arcy is quite equal to the occasion. She looks right through him, and goes on her way without a falter. Captain Stamer, however, happens to be a person of much resource also. He steps lightly in front of her.

"I've had quite a difficulty about finding you," says he. "Ah, how d'ye do?" to Crawford. "But," gaily, "here you are at last."

Miss D'Arcy is so overcome by this audacity that words fail her.

"Been enjoying yourself?" goes on Captain Stamer, with growing geniality, unchecked by the eye she has fixed on him.

"Very much indeed, thank you," stonily.

"So glad. Rather warm day though, isn't it?" turning to walk with them.

"You have not yet told me why you are

here," says Miss D'Arcy, turning at last indignant eyes to his.

"No? Haven't I? I quite thought I had. Marian gave me a message for you to the effect that she would like you to come to her for a moment, if possible. She would have come to you, only——"

"Where is she?"

"Over there, I think," pointing to where a group is gathered at the end of the tennis ground.

"Will you take me to her, Mr. Crawford?" asks Evelyn, turning to him with a smile.

"Certainly," and the three start off together towards the spot on which Miss Vandeleur is supposed to be, Captain Stamer having refused to take his dismissal. Half way there, however, a diversion occurs. From behind a clump of rhododendrons a pretty woman darts forward, and takes possession of Mr. Crawford.

"Here you are," cries Mrs. Wylding-Weekes. "And alive too! Of course I thought you were dead as you never came to take me to see those swans. Hah! Evelyn, I expect I have *you* to thank for his defection. That's one I owe you."

"I'm extremely sorry," says Mr. Crawford composedly. "I can't think how I forgot it. I hope you will excuse me, but——"

"I always excuse everybody," says Mrs. Wylding-Weekes. "I'm bound to—they have always such a lot to excuse in me. And as there is still time for you to redeem your promise, I can't see that I have any grievance. Miss D'Arcy will let you off. Three is trumpery, you know."

She nods blithely at Evelyn ; seizes upon the unwilling Crawford and hauls him off, almost literally before he has time to frame a defence.

It is a little way she has, so nobody minds her much when they have got over the first shock. Her manners are not her strong point, but her face is undeniably pretty in spite of the turned-up nose that adorns the centre of it. Her eyes are bright and sparkling ; her years are few ; her knowledge of mankind large and unlimited ; social laws are as naught to her, and propriety, as considered by the more

sober section of humanity, is a myth. Her
husband, as will be readily understood, is an
entirely secondary person in her *ménage*, and
but for the bursts of jealousy that about once
a week drive him into prominence he would
probably be as good as dead and buried.

So far as her acquaintances go, women, except for one here and there, she vigorously
refuses to cultivate, whilst in her eyes no man,
however undesirable, is without his interest.
Her gowns, the cut, the extraordinary variety
of them, is a never-ending source of scandalous
gossip amongst her set. She hunts in the
season three days a week ; in and out of season
she flirts openly and thoroughly. Her hair is
a bright red ; her hands little models ; need
it be said she plays the banjo. Mr. Wylding-
Weekes being a man of old family and large
means, no one has as yet plucked up courage
to cut her, though her detractors, mostly
women, of course, would gladly have seen a
safe way to doing so. Meanwhile she goes on
her way rejoicing, careless of comment, and
ever eager for the fray. She has one virtue,
however—she is eminently good-natured ; she

has one friend too, of her own sex—Evelyn D'Arcy.

Mr. Crawford being a new man is naturally of supreme importance in her eyes; having impounded him, nothing is left to Evelyn but to continue her way to Marian with Stamer as sole companion.

"For once Mrs. Wylding-Weekes has done me a good turn," says that young man with a laugh.

"Yes?" with unpleasant question in the tone.

"She has sequestrated Crawford—see?"

"No, I don't," immovably.

"Oh, well, *I* do. Horrid old bore, isn't he?"

"I think he is one of the nicest people I ever met."

"You're easily pleased then."

"There is one thing, Eaton, that may as well be said. You have forced your society upon me, and as you *compel* me to endure it, I must beg you not to say uncivil things of people whom I like."

"What on earth is the matter with you?"

demands Captain Stamer, turning sharply round as if to examine her features at leisure. They have entered a laurel walk and are, so long as nobody turns the corner, virtually alone. " Has he taught you to speak like that ? "

" Nobody has taught me anything," says Miss D'Arcy with much spirit. " What I know I have learned from myself, and one thing my inner consciousness has evolved is, that I will let no man, or woman either" (with rising wrath), " speak to me as you have done."

"Look here," says Stamer promptly, "I know what you mean, and I know too that you have every cause to hate me; I should never have said what I did to you, even though I swear I meant nothing uncivil by it. I wouldn't annoy *you*, Evelyn. Well, I apologize ; I was a brute. I will go down on my knees if you like and cry *peccavi*, only make it up with me."

At this Miss D'Arcy, who has been watching him out of the corner of her eye, after a severe struggle with her more dignified self, gives way to mirth.

" You needn't spoil your trousers for *me*,"

says she ; " the whole matter isn't worth a yard of tweed."

" Am I to understand by that, that you——"

" Oh, yes, I forgive you," indifferently.

" Give me your hand on it," says Captain Stamer, and having secured that pretty member, he carries it to his lips and kisses it with an apparently profound gratitude.

" There, that will do," says Miss D'Arcy, shaking him off a little coldly. " Now come, come to Marian ; if indeed," regarding him with sudden doubt, " she ever sent you to seek me."

" She did. She did, I give you my honour," declares he fervently. " You see the prizes are going to be given away, and the duchess——"

" There was no necessity to trouble me about that. The colonel could have got my prize for me."

" It appears the duchess expressed a wish to give it to you in person."

" A fig for the duchess ! " says Miss D'Arcy, with very proper contempt for authority of all sorts. " Do you think I would go out of my

way for ten thousand duchesses? Tut! you
don't know me.   I——"

But at this moment a very charming person
comes round the corner, and Miss D'Arcy, who
had been strong to resist a mighty array of
duchesses, goes down before one lovely face.

"Ah, Marian!" cries she, running to her.

"But where have you been, Evelyn?" says
Miss Vandeleur, in a little vexed way.   As her
vexed ways are always for the good of others,
and never for the good of herself, nobody minds
them.   She is a tall slight girl of about three-
and-twenty, with a singularly attractive face,
not strictly pretty perhaps, but very lovable
and full of dignity; the lips are sweet and
suggestive of repose, of strength; the forehead
is broad, the whole expression gentle, but firm.

"I was coming to you," says Evelyn, "but
—but Eaton tells me the duchess wants to give
me my prize in person, and," nervously, "I
should not like *that*, with everybody looking
on, you know; it—it would be *dreadful;*
couldn't," coaxingly, "couldn't the colonel get
mine for me?"

"No, you must come yourself; the duchess

wants to see you, to be introduced to you.
You really must come, Evelyn," seeing signs
of insubordination in her small friend's face.
" For one thing, it will be a rudeness to refuse,
and for another, she is going to have a large
party at the Castle for tableaux, plays, &c., and
she has asked me to stay there, and she wants
you to stay there also."

" Oh, well, I couldn't, there's an end of it.
I couldn't," says Miss D'Arcy, with actual
horror in her tone. " Are you mad, Marian?
Why," in a whisper, this lest Eaton should
hear, " I haven't a gown fit to be seen. I——"

" Forget all that for the present. You can
refuse her invitation later on if you like ; for
the moment all you have got to do is to come
up to her, take your prize, accept your invitation, and beat a dignified retreat. There,"
laughing, " it isn't so much after all, is it ? "

" No," says Miss D'Arcy, giving in evidently,
but in so heartbroken a tone that both her
companions burst out laughing.

She is borne off forthwith to receive her
prize, a handsome gold bracelet, and to
receive also an invitation to the Castle for the

following week, which she accepts, with Miss
Vandeleur's eye upon her; and presently the
duchess sails away, carrying her train with
her, and everybody else, feeling the day to be
now really at an end, make their adieux to Lady
Stamer, who is looking tired and bored. The
colonel and Mrs. D'Arcy have driven away by
themselves in the rare old article they call a
phaeton, and which would fetch any price at
a fancy sale, Evelyn having declared her intention of walking home. It is a cool, pretty
walk under soft green trees that intertwine
their branches across the road, and one she
loves to take. Eaton Stamer accompanies
her to the entrance gate, and here she stops
him.

"Thus far, and no farther," says she with
just a little ghost of a smile. She has not yet
forgiven him.

"Nonsense. I shall see you home."

"And be late for dinner, and have Lady
Stamer's wrath hurled upon my head. No,
thanks."

"You mean my society is not worth that.
Well, it isn't. But I'll have plenty of time to

take you to Firgrove and come back again to dinner."

"You really must not come," says Evelyn with a cold glance. "I prefer, I much prefer, to return home alone."

"How hard you are," says he, with a wrathful glance at her—"just like a bit of granite. I'll speak to Mr. Vaudrey about you. In my opinion you are in a bad way. People who won't forgive their neighbours are——"

"My dear girl! Is that you? Going home? I quite thought you had gone with the colonel and Mrs. D'Arcy. *So* fortunate. Now I shall have a companion, for your way is mine." The loud and piercing tones of Mrs Vaudrey smite upon the air.

Captain Stamer smothers what—let us hope —is a kindly exclamation.

"Good-bye!" says he, holding out his hand to Evelyn. All hope of a *tête-à-tête* with her is now clearly at an end. "So glad you will have so delightful a companion as Mrs. Vaudrey. One would think "—to that unsuspicious lady —"that you had *known* how I longed for you.

It will be quite a comfort for Evelyn to have some one to talk to on her way home."

" Oh, thanks! thanks!" says Mrs. Vaudrey vaguely. She is staring at him with all her might. " Bless me, Eaton, what's that in your hair?" says she—"just over the tip of your ear."

" *What?*" exclaims he wildly, making violent dabs at the part of his person indicated. *No* one likes to think an earwig or a caterpillar is nesting in one's head.

"There! it's gone," says Mrs. Vaudrey. " After all "—with a careful examination of the ground at her feet—" I believe it was only a bit of twig; but it looked so odd, and I thought it moved. One never can be sure of those insect beasts. Gave you a shock, eh?"

"I daresay I'll recover—after you have gone," says he grimly. He is again holding out his hand to Evelyn. " *Say* you forgive me," whispers he hurriedly, tightening his grasp on hers. As he is plainly filled with a determination to hold her prisoner until pardon is granted, Miss D'Arcy wisely surrenders.

"Yes," says she. It is a bald making-up, but the smile that accompanies the monosyllable more than compensates for the poorness of it.

"Until to-morrow then," says he, lifting his hat. "Good-bye, Mrs. Vaudrey; safe home. I need not wish you better company."

He beams upon that offending lady also, and with a last glance for Evelyn turns back to the house.

CHAPTER XI

"WELL—it went off very well, didn't it?" says Mrs. Vaudrey, stepping out smartly beside Evelyn; one end of her gown is dragging gaily in the dust beside her, but that's nothing here nor there where Mrs. Vaudrey is concerned.

"It was a *lovely* day," says Evelyn, whose spirits have risen unaccountably during the last three minutes. Can it be Mrs. Vaudrey's society that has had this desired effect? Perhaps it was the triumph of having conquered Eaton's determination to go home with her— perhaps it is the Christian satisfaction she ought to feel at having at last forgiven him.

"Well, so-so," says Mrs. Vaudrey, as if hardly pleased at the answer received. "There was a moment when I felt certain we were going to have a shower." It is quite plain that the shower would have received a hearty welcome from *one* of the guests at all events.

"Oh, I'm glad it kept off. Everything was as near to perfection as it could be."

"It was smart, very smart; to do Bessie Stamer justice she certainly *grudges* nothing— that is to her own aggrandizement. And of course she can do things as she likes. No stint, you know; and everything in her own hands. Ha! ha!" with hollow mirth. "I always laugh when I think what a cipher Sir Bertram is. We all speak of his mother's entertainments, whereas in reality they are his."

"He is certainly a very good son," says Evelyn cautiously, who has been over the ground before.

"He's a fool!" says Mrs. Vaudrey with a truly noble disregard of subterfuge. "She gets all the praise, and *he* pays the piper! If he married now——" long pause, filled with hopeful imaginings—"what a change it would be for her. I hope"—with a sudden eagerness that carries her on a yard or two with great speed—"that when he *does* marry his wife will prove a virago!"

"Oh! Poor Sir Bertram," says Evelyn a little startled; "what on earth has he done to you?"

"Nothing! nothing. I wish him no harm. But I hope I shall live to see a mistress at Parklands who will be a match for Bessie. I've known her all my life, as girl and woman, and she wants—well, to be treated as she treats others. Not another word about her, my dear," as though Evelyn has been abusing her unrighteously. "It isn't right that a girl like you should nourish vindictive feelings. Did you see her gown, dear? Handsome, eh?"

"I thought it beautiful," says Evelyn absently. Her mind has flown indeed to other scenes.

"Fifty pounds, if it cost a penny. But too young for her. Did you mark that, Evelyn? Twenty years too young. A girl might have worn it! Absurd in a woman of her age to deck herself out like that. And have you noticed? a young gown on an *old* woman (and Bessie's old if you like) only makes her seem more than her age. Didn't you think she looked specially worn—done up—eh ? "

" I didn't look at her," says Evelyn, who indeed seldom studies Lady Stamer's features.

" Well, she did ; older than she is, though she is fifty-five if a *day ;* she may pose as forty, if she likes, but who is going to believe her ? And at all events," cheerfully, " she can't *look* it, though she may say it. She is ten years older than I am, though you wouldn't think it, eh ? "

" I would," says Evelyn honestly ; and indeed Mrs. Vaudrey, badly gowned and all as she is, does look considerably Lady Stamer's junior.

" No—would you really ? " says that matron, much gratified. " Well, perhaps there *are* people who wear worse. I must say you looked nice to-day, if you like "—this is a delicate return compliment. " I could see the duchess took a tremendous fancy to you, which was by no means agreeable to my Lady Stamer."

" I don't see why she need care," with a slight frown.

" That's just it. It's no affair of hers, yet she *must* interfere. It's all jealousy, my dear, and something else, too, in your case. She is *afraid* of you, my dear."

" Of me? of me? Nonsense!"

" There, there, so be it, as they say at the end of the prayers. But I have my own thoughts, for all that. The duchess was civil to me too, didn't you think? But then her family and ours are old friends; you know all about that, don't you?"

" Yes — all — everything," declares Miss D'Arcy with the vehemence of despair, yet hardly hoping thereby to stem the torrent. Nevertheless this time she escapes a rehearsal of the relations that once existed between the Saintons and her grace. Mrs. Vaudrey, providentially, has let that thing she is pleased to call her mind run upon more immediate matters.

" Bessie's face was a picture when she came up and found me receiving her ' august guest' —that's what she calls her, I'll be bound. Did you see her? Ha—ha—ha!" There is genuine, if malicious, mirth in her note this

time. "She was *green*. The duchess disap-
proved of her gown; I could see that at a
glance. Altogether too juvenile. But poor
Bessie never could understand the date called
yesterday. Thinks herself always young and
beautiful; she's *hideous*, to my eyes. That
hooked nose of hers would condemn her anywhere."

"She could never have been even good-
looking," says Evelyn with conviction, to
whom, as we know, Lady Stamer is abhorrent.

"No, neither bodily nor mentally. And to
see her strutting about in that gown. Well!
One shouldn't talk about it; any one listening
—except you, my dear, who know me—might
think I was jealous of it. But as for me——.
However, one can't help thinking how fortunate she is. Look at my gown, now, for
example, such a contrast to hers, yet I am
better born than ever she was. "This"—
pulling out the ancient skirt with a vigour
that makes Evelyn shudder for the duration
of it —"is its fourth summer; it has been
dyed once, turned twice. And not so bad
after all, is it?"

She pauses here with such a triumphant air, that Miss D'Arcy has not the heart to refrain from lying.

"It looks very nice," says she.

"It is wonderful—really quite a grand old skirt, *I* call it, after Gladstone, don't you know. It has stood to me, in season and out of it. Nothing like getting a *good* material when you are about it."

"It is economy," says Evelyn, "only somehow we never have the money to get the good material."

"Well, I don't suppose I ever shall again," says Mrs. Vaudrey, "now the children are getting so big. But, however, *this*"—touching the heirloom again—"will last me for a good bit yet on high days and holidays. But it does seem hard, doesn't it, that Bessie should have so many good gowns when I have only one? And I wouldn't care about that either if she wasn't so——. Good gracious!"—breaking off suddenly—"what a vindictive eye she has. A key to the soul, my dear. Between you and me," pushing her hand through Evelyn's arm and speaking in a tragic whisper—"she's a *snake !*"

"Oh, no," says Evelyn.

"Yes, she is. She's a snake. Who should know her if I didn't? She 'smiles and smiles, and is at heart a villain.'" She makes this remarkable assertion triumphantly, being evidently under the impression that she is quoting Shakespeare correctly.

"I don't really think she is as bad as that," says Evelyn, rather startled.

"She is though. She is a regular snake in the grass! As if I didn't understand her. I *should*. She is my worst enemy; yet I have done that woman ever so many good turns from time to time—long ago, I mean, when she, the squire's daughter, was glad to know the daughter of a baron. Not that I boast, Evelyn. I should hope I'm above *that* sort of thing. But it *is* galling, you know."

"It is, I suppose," says Evelyn, with deep sympathy.

"One would think I was the last person in the world she feels envy about, but it seems it is not so. She envies me my influence in the village ; she envies me my old women, who, goodness knows, aren't worth that or anything else, ungrateful old wretches ! She would undermine me if she could. See how she acted the other day about that coal fund."

" She acted abominably," says Miss D'Arcy, who is a partizan of the first water, and besides has wrongs of her own to remember.

" It seems impossible that she should grudge me the little I have got. She, who has everything in the world—position, money, and good sons, too, though I don't like Sir Bertram's eye — *knowing*, *I* call it — and what have I got ? Only the children, and the old parishioners, and—well, yes," as if admitting something against her better judgment, "Reginald, of course."

Reginald is Mr. Vaudrey.

" You could have no better possession than Mr. Vaudrey," cries Evelyn quickly.

" Yes, my dear," placidly ; " I quite agree with you. But he's poor, you know, He," thoughtfully, " is the poorest person I know.

We never have a penny we can squander
comfortably, like other people, and that's a
great drawback, you know.   One likes to
squander occasionally.   It is in the blood.
But squandering and we, are two."

"Yes, that's the way with us, too," says
Evelyn, shaking her charming head with quite
a melancholy air.

"And how different it is with her—Bessie
Stamer, I mean.   Of course she comes of a
good family.   No one is saying a word against
that.   County people they were.   The Dain-
trys, you know, of Warwick.   But—well, one
shouldn't talk of it."

"Why not?" says Evelyn, with commend-
able courage, knowing Mrs. Vaudrey will talk
of it, in spite of her words to the contrary.
"You mean that your father——"

"Just so, my dear.   She was a commoner
—I was not.   But my father, Lord Sainton,
hadn't a *sou*.   He was, I remember, delighted
when Mr. Vaudrey proposed to me.   One off
his shoulders, don't you see?   A mouth less
to feed and clothe."

"And you—was it to oblige your father

that you married Mr. Vaudrey?" asks Evelyn, a touch of indignation in her tone.

"N—o, my dear. Honestly, I think not. It seems absurd, now, Evelyn, doesn't it? but really I believe there was a time when I was dreadfully in love with Mr. Vaudrey."

"I should think you would be dreadfully in love with him now, too," says Evelyn, with a slight increase of the indignation.

"Oh, well—as to that!" says Mrs. Vaudrey with a most unromantic laugh. "There—you mightn't think it," says she, as if starting a regular problem, difficult of solution, "but there was a time when I used to think Reginald was absolutely *handsome!*" Poor Reginald! Years and worries, and frettings over his destitutes, have left him far from handsome now, save in the eyes of those who can appreciate him. It angers Evelyn that his nearest and dearest should take him thus baldly, but after all no man is a prophet in his own country.

"He has a beautiful face always," says she, with a little lump in her throat, as she sees rise before her mind's eye the vicar's, pale, eager, emaciated features ; his great unworldly eyes, his stoop, the unsatisfied longings that life has left so clearly stamped upon him.

"There are uglier, certainly," says Mrs. Vaudrey, pursing up her lips, as if with a desire to give him and all men fair play.

"He is the best man in the world," says Evelyn vehemently.

"He is," agrees his wife placidly. "*Too* good. I wish," with a heartfelt sigh, "he had a little less goodness, and a little more coin of the realm."

"You can't mean that," says Evelyn, who after all is *very* young.

"*Can't* I ?" with deep feeling. "I do, though. And I wish he had a little more common sense into the bargain. I don't mind talking to you, Evelyn—you are one of the most reasonable girls I know, though you *are* good-looking, and I say that if you were in my shoes you would wish Mr. Vaudrey different to. He is a saint, if you like, but one fares lenten-wise all the year round when attached to that class, and one tires of bread without butter *always*. Why can't he think? Is to-morrow of no consequence? Surely he needn't give *all* to the poor."

" Not all, of course."

" No. Even Abraham did not go so far as that. A little of all that he possessed satisfied *him*. But Mr. Vaudrey wants to out-Cæsar Cæsar. Now look here, Evelyn! You will admit, I suppose, that every gentleman must have at least two suits of clothes."

" At the least."

" One suit for Sundays, and one for week-days. Well, that is just what I can't make Mr. Vaudrey take to heart. Up comes one of the parishioners—old Hodgson for choice if you like—complaining of his eternal sciatica or lumbago, or whatever ridiculous disorder may be rife in the parish at the time ; and on the instant Mr. Vaudrey falls a victim to his wiles, and gives him, without a thought, his second-best breeches. After that, of what use is the second-best coat and waistcoat, I want to know? Of none—of none at all, and no-thing therefore is left him but to give his Sunday suit to his Monday's work. That's imperative, Evelyn. You know a man can't go visiting all over the parish in a coat and waistcoat only."

" No! no," says Evelyn regretfully. She is evidently seriously annoyed with the present state of our moral laws. A coat and waistcoat *only!* No, they would never sanction that. She is troubled too with an awful inward vision of her pastor and master, careering wildly down the village street, clad in the scanty habiliments Mrs. Vaudrey has so graphically pictured. Would the children hunt him? the dogs? It is a terrible bit of imagery! She pales before it.

"Oh! he ought *not* to give away his trousers," says she, almost tearfully.

"I knew you would see it as I do," returns Mrs. Vaudrey, well pleased. " But he's a fool, my dear—Reginald is a regular fool. One would think he was a millionaire the way he goes on. Yet he never has a decent rag to his back, and not an ounce of flesh on his bones."

"He does look thin," says Miss D'Arcy, calling up the vicar's cadaverous face. " Does he," falteringly—" does he *eat* enough? Has he a good appetite?"

" Enormous!" says Mrs. Vaudrey with considerable energy. "He eats like a trooper. More than I do with all the children thrown in. There again, my dear Evelyn, you can see how expensive it is to marry a really good man. If he would doze away an hour or two of his day in his study, pretending to write his sermons, you know, or studying the Ancient Fathers, a *mild* luncheon might satisfy him, but all that trudging through the keen air from morning till night, to see how his poor are getting on, gives him an appetite before which an alderman might quail."

Evelyn sighs, with a sense of relief.

" Why didn't he come to Parklands to-day?" asks she.

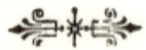

CHAPTER XII

"My dear girl, *need* you ask? Old Betty Whinsdale has a touch of the 'rheumatics,' and wanted a prayer said over her. As a *charm*, believe me; but of course Mr. Vaudrey thinks it was an excess of religion on her part, and so he has given his day to her. Besides, he wasn't fit to be seen. Martin Tweedy got the second-best trousers last Sunday week, and now Reginald's best clothes aren't good enough for a duchess! Besides—between you and me and the wall—he doesn't like Bessie."

"Surely, surely," indignantly, "she could not have been rude to *him*."

"Couldn't she? That's all *you* know about it. Now I know very well all Mr. Vaudrey's faults, but I tell you this, Evelyn," a deep red mounting to her brow, "that the person who could wilfully say a word to wound him, must be essentially *bad*. He wouldn't tell me about

it, but I found it out.   It was about his early
celebrations.   You know how he takes to
heart any little sneer about that part of his
ministry, and Lady Stamer no doubt knows it
too; anyhow she offended him.   I suppose,"
bitterly, "she wanted to get rid of him; he
was not well dressed enough for her dinner-
parties.   His evening suit is shabby, I know,
and where on earth is he to get seven guineas
to buy another?   Besides, he was always asking her for money for his charities, and she
hates giving.   But it was his shabbiness above
all things that annoyed her.   She—— I
declare to you, Evelyn," breaking off suddenly
to seize her companion's arm, and walking her
almost into a run in her excitement, "there are
moments when I wish I was Lucrezia Borgia
or some such enterprising person, that I might
poison that woman."

"I don't see what you would gain by it,"
says Evelyn, who is fast getting out of
breath.

"Don't you?   I'd gain the loss of her, for
one thing.   However," with pious hope in tone
and look, "she can't have it all her own way

for ever. The time will come when she will find she is not as clever as she thinks. She'll be foiled sooner or later. For one thing," with a glance at Evelyn, "I don't believe that pet scheme of hers will come off."

"What scheme?" indifferently.

"As if you didn't know," says Mrs. Vaudrey, giving her a playful, if somewhat hurtful dig in the ribs.

"Well, I don't!" says Miss D'Arcy rather shortly. Nobody likes a severe pain in the side.

"What! Not about Marian Vandeleur?"

"About Marian?"

"Who else, in Heaven's name? She's the only one round here with a penny to her fortune."

"I'm still all abroad," says Evelyn, throwing out her pretty hands expressively.

"You mean to tell me honestly that you didn't know?" exclaims Mrs. Vaudrey, coming to a sudden standstill, and reading the girl's face as though she would compel the truth to lie there in open print.

"I think I've been telling you that for the

past five minutes," says Evelyn a little impatiently.

"Then you are the one ignorant person in Fenton. All the world knows that she has set her heart on marrying Eaton to Marian Vandeleur!"

There is a slight pause, whilst the girl, who has come to a standstill too, gazes into the woman's eyes.

"Oh, no! Oh, that is ridiculous! That will never be," says Evelyn at last, with a curious, thoughtless vehemence.

"That's what I say. It will never be. She won't be able to manage *that*—eh?" with a meaning side glance at her companion, that is completely thrown away.

"And yet—why not?" says the girl very slowly, and with an expression on her face as though she is looking inward and backward on her life's short journey. "Why should they *not* marry? It would be a good match for both. Marian is the dearest girl I know, and Eaton——" the pause is eloquent. "He will suit her—I think—perhaps."

"Perhaps!" says Mrs. Vaudrey drily, giving

her a shrewd glance. "What a hypocrite you are, Evelyn! Of course I know girls are never honest about these things, but to me, an old friend—I——"

"What things?"

"Oh, there! If you won't you won't, you know. But that one should be all at once deaf, and dumb, and blind, is asking a good deal. However, no matter. The principal thing is, that you agree with me, that Bessie will be frustrated in this one matter at least. Here's the stile, my dear. Here we part. It is my short cut to the Vicarage. As for you, you haven't a dozen more yards to go."

"Even if I had I should enjoy it—the evening is so lovely," says Evelyn. "Good-bye. Give my love to the vicar and to the children, and send up the two young ones to see us to-morrow, if you can manage it."

"I'll be delighted to manage it," says Mrs. Vaudrey cheerfully. "And it is always such a treat to them to go to you."

She kisses Evelyn, steps lightly on to the stile, poises on the top step a moment, turns to say a last airy word, and overbalancing her

portly frame comes with an undesirable speed
to the grass on the other side.

"Oh! are you *hurt?*" cries Evelyn in an
agony.

"Not a bit—not a bit!" exclaims she,
scrambling to her feet once more. "But my
good gown, my dear"—making anxious examination of it over her shoulders at the im-
minent risk of giving herself a lasting crick in
her neck—"what of it? Not spoiled, eh?"

"Not a soil," says Evelyn. "It is as good
as ever it was," which, after all, isn't saying
much for it.

Mrs. Vaudrey, comforted, however, goes on
her way rejoicing, with a last buoyant wave
of her hand.

Evelyn, having watched her cross the next
field—with the beloved skirts so high upheld
as to show a considerable amount of ankles of
truly noble proportions—and tackle the second
stile without further mishap, resumes her own
way.

As she does so, a quick sigh escapes her.
She is conscious too of a feeling of irritation
difficult of suppression. What had Mrs.

Vaudrey meant by calling her a hypocrite?
What had she to do with the failure or
success of Lady Stamer's scheme for her
son's aggrandizement? If she thought——she
checks herself here, and an angry, offended
blush dyes her face. Why should she have
thought it? Why should any one dare to
think it? What was Eaton to her but an old
friend—a brother almost? But Mrs. Vaudrey,
in spite of her undeniable good birth, was
always a little odd—a little *vulgar.* Nobody
should mind anything she said, And after all,
what did it matter?

Her cheeks are still very hot, however,
when just at her own gate she meets the vicar,
swinging along in that strange loose way of
his, with his chin in the air, and his eyes
dreaming—of heaven, perhaps.

"You—you, my dear—*you!*" says he, in the
queer confused way natural to him, and that
is always so suggestive of a person just roused
from some engrossing thoughts.

"Yes. I am only now returning from the
garden party at Parklands," says she, smiling
at him. "You were not there?"

" No, no.   I could not manage it," says the vicar, patting the little hand he holds.   "It was pleasant?   You enjoyed yourself?   Ah, right—right.   Pleasure is always for the young."

" It is for you too—if you would have it," says she almost reproachfully.

" Why, so I do have it," says he, as if surprised at her words.   " I am specially happy to-day, for example, though I did not go to Lady Stamer's *fête*.   You know old Betty Whinsdale?   Well, then, you know too how hard she is to—to influence ; but to-day——" he stops, and looks at Evelyn with an almost eager light in his large eyes—" to-day, I think she *felt*—at last," says he, with a long sigh of thankfulness.

It is quite impossible for Evelyn, who knows the man—and Betty—not to wonder secretly what he has given the old woman to-day, Betty's pieties being lax or strong according to the value of the gifts bestowed.   With that last conversation with Mrs. Vaudrey still fresh within her mind, she is conscious of casting a furtive glance at his clothing, and it is with a positive feeling of relief that she sees that all his garments are upon him.

"That has made you happy," says she softly. Not for worlds would she have cast a doubt on Betty's purity of purpose.

"That—and other things. I went from her to Hodgson's, and there—found a regular transformation scene. You know who has been at work in this parish of late, don't you, Evelyn? You know Mr. Crawford?"

"Yes. Is it he——"

"He is a good man," says the vicar, interrupting her with some glad excitement. "He is indeed a Christian, both in thought and act. His charity is unbounded. Those people were reduced to the verge of starvation—all I could do for them would not have staved off the evil hour much longer—when he, Mr. Crawford, came to the rescue. Without a word to any man he set them up again. I was never so astonished as when I arrived at their miserable home. I—I confess to you, my dear girl, that it was with lagging steps I drew near to it, for I hadn't a penny in my pocket, and what words, even if taken from sacred writ, can comfort the poor soul whose stomach is empty? Well, when I entered, there was the fire burning, a pot boiling on it, out of which came a goodly steam—a *handsome* one, I can tell you," says the vicar, with an irrepressible laugh, "and the children all clustered round the fire, in happy expectation, and the mother, poor creature, looking ten years younger. 'Who had done it?' I asked. 'Mr. Crawford!' And all through a word of mine let fall to him last week. He has taken on Hodgson, too, at regular wages, and is giving him work suited to his weak state of health. Truly," says Mr. Vaudrey, the tears rising in his eyes, "God did well when he made Crawford wealthy."

"Oh, how good it was of him! I cannot tell you how I like him," says Evelyn with a little burst of enthusiasm.

"He has a heart above the average. He not only gives, but he loves giving. He is such a help to me as I never hoped to find. Sir Bertram is very good, but he doesn't enter into it with me. *This* man has sympathy," says the poor vicar gratefully, thinking of all the years he has toiled during which no man

cared whether he gained a soul or lost it.
"He has the true spirit. He gives with both
hands, and with all his heart. He seems to
long to give."

"I know," says Evelyn. "Once or twice it
has occurred to me that he must have some
reason for his great generosity towards the
poor and suffering. Could he ever have been
poor himself—and wanted help and love?"

"I don't know. That idea didn't suggest
itself to me. But rather that perhaps some
one belonging to him—his father, it might
be—had committed some wrong, and he was
trying to expiate it. As for himself, I believe
he is incapable of wronging any one."

"Quite," says Evelyn with conviction. "His
face is both gentle and sad. Mr. Vaudrey,
did you ever see so sad a face? He makes me
always feel so dreadfully sorry for him. And
if he is expiating the sins of others, how dear
of him. How few men care for anything
that doesn't concern themselves."

"Well, it is all mere surmise," says the
vicar. "And why should we not believe that
his unbounded charities arise from nothing

but a sincere desire to follow the steps of his Redeemer? I *must* think he loves the poor, so zealous is he for their welfare. Those Meesons, now—he asked me about them, and now, thanks to him, they too are in a fair way towards prosperity, and that boy of theirs recovering rapidly."

"Tom Meeson?"

"Yes. We thought there was no hope. But Mr. Crawford, when he had been to see him once or twice, did not agree with me. It appears he has dabbled in medicine. And he would not hear of having the dispensary doctor. He sent the whole way to Darlton for Jones—you know how successful Jones is; and indeed he has done wonders for Tom."

"His coming here has been a great comfort to you," says Evelyn, looking with pleasure at the vicar's brilliant eyes, now so full of glad· ness. His worn face is lighted up; his whole person seems to have taken on a new sense of satisfaction and certain hope for the future. It is characteristic of the man that all this new-found delight is not for himself but for his poor.

"It is the relief," says he simply. "The freedom from care. The knowledge that there is some one I can rely upon to help me, when times are bad. Yes, Crawford is a good man, and an honest friend to the poor. He not only desires to help them, but he *feels* for them. Good-bye, my dear. God bless you! I'm in a hurry home. To confess the truth to you, I'm starving with hunger."

Here he laughs gaily, and swings away down the road, to stop a moment after to call back to her: "Your father? your mother? quite well, I hope?"

Years have not compelled him to remember that the colonel is only her uncle and Mrs. D'Arcy her aunt.

"Quite well, thank you," returns Evelyn with a little nod. Then he turns the corner and is gone.

CHAPTER XIII

It is the next morning, and Lady Stamer's day at home. She has consented to sacrifice one day in the week to her acquaintances, but woe and betide those, who, coming to her on that special afternoon, are considered by her outside the pale of society. Just at first the doctor's wife and the country attorney's had ventured to present themselves on the day on which she has declared herself ready and willing to receive all visitors. They came once—they came never again. Lady Stamer in one lesson gave them their level—in plain language she taught them in a single interview how altogether beneath notice they were, and how many fathoms deep they lay under that delectable social circle of which she reigned the queen. To achieve this she had to be excessively rude, which, of course, considering her birth, must, or at all events ought, to have been abhorrent to her. She must have had a strong mind, however, as she betrayed no symptoms of remorse, then, or afterwards.

In Fenton she was in effect the ruler of society, as there was no resident lord within forty miles of it; and the one or two other baronets who had places in the neighbourhood were by no means so well off as Sir Bertram.

In the beginning, after his father's death, she had affected to withdraw from all supervision of the household, but a word from Sir Bertram had been sufficient to reinstate her in all her old privileges. As a fact she now ruled Parklands with a rod of iron—the very owner of it coming sometimes beneath the despotic government that was detested by all who lived beneath it.

The owner of this lovely estate was, however —odd to say—the favourite with his mother. For Eaton, the second son, she had hardly ever felt those maternal pangs that as a rule accompany such love. When the latter was born she felt he was one too many. Her ambition was her strongest point, and having contracted an heir to Parklands, she had felt

that anything further was worse than useless—
was in effect a drain upon the resources that
should have gone in their entirety to feed the
fortunes of the future master of the place.   It
was fortunate that no other children blessed,
or as she would have thought marred, her
married lot; the small amount of attention
she bestowed upon her second child would
probably have lessened into absolute neglect
of a third or fourth.   She was indeed one of
those many women whom nature meant to be
childless; she had neither the love to give
them nor the knowledge that such love should
be given.   But nature sometimes is at fault.

By this time the morning has deepened
into noon.   It is well into June now, and all
the loveliest flowers of England are blooming
in the pretty beds that Lady Stamer has had
laid out beneath the drawing-room windows.
These glowing flowers are even the lovelier
because of the growth of their later sisters
beside them—the now half-budding plants
that in the near July will send their fragrance
up to heaven.   It is as though we have now
before us, clasped together, the life that is

almost over and the life to come. Despair
and hope in one breath!

"Yes, I think the duchess *was* pleased,"
says Lady Stamer complacently, with a sort
of after-glow that heightens her smile and her
colour, but which she fondly believes is unknown to any one. "It was so perfect a day."

"Not a hitch," says Mrs. Vaudrey, who has
dropped in, and who, however martial behind
her back, shows only a smothered hostility
when in presence of Lady Stamer—unless
indeed occasion calls for combat.

"I meant the weather," says Lady Stamer.
She stares at Mrs. Vaudrey through the long-
handled *pince-nez* that hangs by her side.

"Well, there's often a hitch in the weather,"
says Mrs. Vaudrey aggressively.

"Everybody played very well, I thought,"
says Miss Vandeleur pleasantly, as though
with a desire to put an end to the hostilities,
that are already in a fair way to make open
war.

"Especially Miss D'Arcy," says Bartholomew
Blount, who unfortunately is present. If he
is the possessor of any talent, it is that of

always saying the right thing in the wrong place.

"A little wild goat like that would be sure to play well," says Lady Stamer with the keenest contempt.

"And what do you say to Lady Flora Grant?" asks Miss Vandeleur good-humouredly. "*She* cannot certainly be called wild in any sense of the word, and yet she plays if possible better than Evelyn."

"Hardly better," says Captain Stamer, who is handing a cup of tea to Marian at the moment.

"Ah! you are a partizan," says she in a low tone, glancing up at him with a smile. He shakes his head, lifts his brows as if in repudiation of the idea, yet looks distinctly pleased nevertheless. Her championship of Evelyn at the desired moment has perhaps made him feel, if possible, more friendly towards her. Poor Evelyn, whose little unconventional ways are so often under discussion.

He is a slightly-built young man, of good height, with his head well set upon his shoulders. There is nothing very special about him, and yet there is hardly an acquaintance of his who has not what is called "a good word" for him. Some little virtue he has about him that renders him popular with most people—geniality might explain it, but genuineness would be nearer still. He is liked because men feel that when he betrays a liking for them he thoroughly means it. He has a kindly face, open eyes, a hearty laugh—all sure passports to favour. No one could call him a beauty, but on the other hand no one would certainly ever call him anything but a gentleman.

"The duchess's house-party threatens to be rather a medley," says Lady Stamer, addressing a Mrs. Coventry, the wife of a neighbouring squire, who has just dropped in. As Miss Coventry has been one of those invited to spend the coming week at the Castle, her mother does not take this with a smiling face.

"You mean——?" says she, hesitating purposely, and looking at Lady Stamer through half-closed lids.

"That all sorts and conditions of people

have been bidden," says Lady Stamer, who is ignorant of Miss Coventry's invitation.

" That is a rather pronounced assertion, don't you think?" says her visitor with a cold smile. " You of course object to somebody who has been asked ?"

" To several," says Lady Stamer, with a shrug of her shoulders.

" The duchess *will* be sorry, if she hears it," says Mrs. Vaudrey with a light laugh ; in which, after the faintest hesitation, Mrs. Coventry joins. The latter is a woman of proportions so ample that one wonders how she has so bitter a tongue.

" The duchess probably will hear it," says Lady Stamer, looking at Mrs. Vaudrey. " And I can only hope so. It will help her to make no such foolish mistakes when next she comes to this county. I hear that little D'Arcy girl is one of the fortunate ones invited to this motley gathering."

" Yes," says Miss Vandeleur gently. " I was glad about that. It will be such a change for her."

" A change indeed," says Lady Stamer,

with a low, insolent laugh. "Eaton, Marian perhaps will take some more tea."

"I'm getting her some," says Sir Bertram. He is always so silent a man that as a rule everybody looks at him when he does speak. He is a good deal older than his brother, who is just twenty-seven, and is so tall, and so broad in proportion, as to command immediate attention into whatsoever room he may enter.

"Colonel D'Arcy is charming," says Mrs. Coventry; "I cannot think why it is that people so run down his daughter."

"His niece," corrects Mrs. Vaudrey.

"Ah! is it so? I always thought she was his daughter."

"They intend you to think so," says Lady Stamer meaningly. "It is evident that they all wish she never *had* had a father."

"Oh, I see—something unpleasant, eh?"

"Very, I should say. If you even mention the word 'father' before the girl, they all redden up, and throw out signs of confusion. Very unpleasant, *I* should call it. Forgery, I should imagine, or some low crime like that."

"Surely this is also what Mrs. Coventry has just now called a 'rather pronounced assertion,'" says Mrs. Vaudrey. "Evelyn's father may have been a failure, without being exactly a criminal."

"He may!" says Lady Stamer, turning aside to adjust the rose in the glass near her, and succeeding in giving everybody present the impression that Mrs. Vaudrey is a person not worth arguing with. Mrs. Vaudrey, driven to forget her politics by this touch of insolence, comes boldly to the front.

"I think Evelyn D'Arcy as charming a girl as I know," says she, with a determination that makes her voice over-loud.

"Marian will take that as a compliment," says Lady Stamer, smiling.

"I do indeed," says Miss Vandeleur, in her gentle, dignified way. "I, too, think Evelyn very charming."

"Charity is your forte, my dear Marian. No doubt you will have your reward here-after. I must say, in espousing the cause you have now in hand, you are earning it honestly. For my part, what any one can see in that little, wild, untutored creature is more than I can imagine. *Such* manners!"

"Very pretty manners, surely," says Miss Vandeleur.

"By pretty, I presume you mean amusing," says Lady Stamer. "Now-a-days, everything is given up to the clowns of society; we bow down before them. 'Make me laugh and I will place you on a pedestal,' is the cry. Good manners, respectability—all give place to this insane desire for amusement. To *my* thinking—old fashioned, no doubt—it seems a pity that some one does not take that girl in hand and re-model her all through."

"That would be a pity indeed," says Marian, as gently as ever. "She has the charm of being quite natural. I hope no one will try to chain her down to bald conventionalities. Such a little, lovely wild-flower as she is, with such a good heart! She feels for all the world. As for her manners, we speak of her as unconventional, but surely yesterday, when she was accepting the duchess's invitation, her words, her air were perfect."

"You should have been a man, Marian,

and a philanthropist, you would have made excellent speeches," says Lady Stamer, without acidity. The young mistress of Riversdale is a person to be cultivated, encouraged, *annexed*, if possible. To make her the wife of her second son, Eaton, is at present Lady Stamer's strongest desire ; Mrs. Vaudrey had not been romancing when she gave Evelyn D'Arcy a hint of this. Had either Marian or Sir Bertram betrayed any liking for each other, Lady Stamer would willingly have given all her energies to the furtherance of a marriage between *them*. But Sir Bertram, beyond a common civility, has been to Marian as he has been to all the world since his coming of age, and Marian of late has been almost cold to him.

" A philanthropist, Marian, is a person who looks down on everybody else, and makes himself whilst on earth very unusually unpleasant to all his neighbours. He generally lives long, and is very little regretted. The nation, on his death, raises a hideous monument to his memory as a token of gratitude to the Heaven who has removed him. That's a speech, if you like," says Mr. Blount, nodding triumphantly at Lady Stamer, his aunt. He is perhaps the one person in the world who finds in Lady Stamer a large fund of amusement. He is also, perhaps, the one person in the world whose quips and cranks do not annoy her.

"In spite of Bartholomew's eloquence, a philanthropist's is a noble cast," says Lady Stamer, as if following out her argument with Marian; "but one sometimes productive of little good, as in this case, my dear Marian. You *may* blind yourself, you cannot hope to blind all the world."

"If I'm to be considered part of the world, I confess I'm blind, too," says Mrs. Vaudrey, who is plainly now in an antagonistic spirit. To please Lady Stamer is generally her object when setting forth to pay a visit to her, but this noble determination wanes and waxes feeble towards the termination of it. "I think that child delicious."

"Ah!" says Lady Stamer, with a peculiar air. She utters this eloquent monosyllable with a sigh of deepest meaning; it conveys to her listeners the knowledge that, so far as she can judge, Mrs. Vaudrey's opinion is beneath notice.

"You don't agree with me?" says Mrs. Vaudrey, who, when at close quarters, is not afraid of her, having a courage of her own. She even manages a smile, so maddened is she by the other's impertinence.

"No," says Lady Stamer, in a stolid tone that admits of no compromise.

"Good heavens! we are in for it. Any short cut anywhere?" asks Mr. Blount, appealing to Sir Bertram in a low tone full of heartfelt despair. Eaton, who is standing near his brother, answers for him.

"Not one," says he ruthlessly. "We are all going to see this matter through. *Hush!* the opposition is making itself heard."

And, indeed, Mrs. Vaudrey is doing her best.

"How strange it is," says she, with an awful sweetness, " that some people never can get accustomed to change—the inevitable change that makes life bearable. A certain groove catches them, and holds them prisoners for ever. They have known such and such people all their lives, and therefore cannot believe that such and such *other* people may have their place upon the same earth as theirs. I state an extreme case, but extreme cases are to be found. But that one should find an example in you, dear Lady Stamer, is indeed a blow."

All this is delivered with peculiar sweetness.

"I hope it won't shatter you," says Lady Stamer, with a benevolence that reduces Mrs. Vaudrey's effort in that line to the level of ordinary good nature.

Mrs. Coventry, who had been talking to Eaton Stamer, but who is now unattached, leans back in her fauteuil and laughs aloud.

"What I meant," says Mrs. Vaudrey, whose anger is now red hot, "was that I should have thought you more liberal than to be the foe of a little girl like Evelyn. You may not like her, but you might at least condone her faults, if she has any. That you should publicly condemn her has shocked me; I confess I expected better things from you."

"Yes?" says Lady Stamer unmoved. "You

are hopeful. Now there are people of whom
I *never* expect anything."

"The colonel, at all events, is a jolly old
soul—like old King Cole," interposes Mr.
Blount, who is great in nursery rhymes, and
who is wise enough to be aware that there
are breakers ahead. He says this with the
kindly intention of leading the conversation
into safer waters. It is a truly self-sacrificing
effort on his part, as a fracas is dear to his
soul, and here seems as pretty an opening as
one need desire for a brisk and lively fray.
He is indeed only led into these peaceable
paths because of the sudden anxious light
that has shown itself in Eaton's eyes. He
crushes his longings, therefore, but all to no
purpose. In spite of him, he has his reward
for his self-denial.

"Colonel D'Arcy is an Irishman," says
Lady Stamer ; she might have spoken volumes,
and yet said less. Her disgust is apparent to
everybody.

"Well, what of that ? " says Mrs. Coventry,
settling herself more squarely in her chair.
Her mother was an Irishwoman of very old

family, and Mrs. Coventry was not now going to be ashamed of her. She, in fact, prided herself on the fact that she had Celtic blood in her veins. Two or three of the young Coventrys have given signs of genius, and this has all been accredited to their maternal grandmother.

"You must really excuse me from going into it," says Lady Stamer in a bored tone. She draws a little gold-topped scent bottle towards her, and unscrewing the stopper sniffs at it plaintively.

"Oh! how shockingly illiberal," cries Mrs. Vaudrey, with a ·playfulness that is only skin deep. "Now, as for me, I adore the poor dear Irish. I think them delightful. So fresh, don't you know, so inconsequent, so out-at-elbows——"

"Oh, it isn't that," says Lady Stamer, with a lazy movement of her fan. "If that was all, one might condone their faults. One is accustomed to that sort of thing. One has to put up with it perpetually. I assure you, my dear Mrs. Vaudrey, that they are not the *only* people I know who are 'out-at-elbows,' as you so—er—so very *feelingly* describe it."

Every one in the room regards this as being unpardonable, the Vaudreys being notoriously hard up, without the remotest chance of ever being less so. A faint pink tinge creeps into Mrs. Vaudrey's sallow cheek, and Eaton Stamer seeing it, loses his temper.

CHAPTER XIV

HE comes forward from behind the curtains of the window, where he has been idly playing with his mother's lap-dog; he is a trifle paler than usual, and his eyes are brilliant.

"How paltry a thing it is, this everlasting denunciation of the 'poor' man," says he with a sneer. He addresses no one in particular, but for a second he lets his eye rest on his mother. "What can money have to do with the man himself? It can neither lift nor lower his morality. There is something vulgar in the dislike to poverty that some people profess. Money is not everything. Heaven has granted to the comparative poor ones of society many compensations. The most charming people I have known have not been amongst the merchant princes of the world. They have had but light acquaintance with purple and fine linen, but they have had in exchange for that goodly raiment, kind hearts and perfect manners—advantages that many rich friends of mine do not possess."

He has been pulling the little dog's ears all the time he has been speaking, and the little creature has been making vigorous efforts to kiss him in return. Now he drops it without a word of warning into Mrs. Vaudrey's lap, who gives a jump, and says, "Oh, my!" as naturally as possible.

This outburst of his has been regarded by his mother, and justly, as a direct attack upon herself, and she resents it accordingly. To her mind it had been provoked by that allusion to Colonel D'Arcy made a few minutes ago, but as a fact, it was her unkind allusion to the Vaudreys' poverty that had provoked it. It was Mrs. Vaudrey's part he had taken, though it might be perhaps a question as to whether he would have been so ready to avenge her had the D'Arcys' name not been mentioned.

Lady Stamer's cold smile has followed every word of her son's utterance. She has seemed even to admire him. It is plain, at all events, that he has amused her. If he had hoped to disconcert her, he has been utterly at fault.

" *Is* he not in earnest? " says she, turning to Mrs. Coventry with quite a glowing smile for her. " Is he not quite like one of his own enchanting beggars, whom he has just been sketching to us, with so able a tongue, when he thus lets himself go? My dear Eaton, this is a surprise—a most gratifying one. You are generally so silent, when with me at all events, that I had no idea you could be so eloquent. And all about nothing too, that is the chief charm, the real cleverness of it. Now if you took a subject of burning moment in hand——"

" If he went into Parliament," suggests Mrs. Coventry, smiling at him.

" True. There is no reason why he should not, some day. You really should think of it, my dear Eaton. To be able to ' orate ' as you do (to use an American word), without a second's preparation, is to be indeed gifted. You are nearly as eloquent as Marian; that should be a bond between you. If ever he goes into Parliament, Marian, you, as an old friend, must promise to help him with his address to his constituents."

"Smart," says Mrs. Vaudrey to herself, "but not smart enough. He will not marry Marian."

"A poor help," says Miss Vandeleur, smiling.

"An excellent one, I should say, and he too, unless his judgment is warped beyond redemption. But about the D'Arcys; we were talking of Colonel D'Arcy, were we not?"

She has deliberately brought up the subject again, knowing that Eaton writhes beneath it, for one thing to punish him for what she styles his insolence, for another to show him that she will not be put down by him or any other.

"Yes, yes, we were," says Mr. Blount mildly. "We were all agreeing, I think, that he is one of the most agreeable people we know."

"Were we?" says Lady Stamer, transfixing him with her glasses. "Put me out of the 'all,' please. For my part, I think his manners and those of his family generally, leave a great deal to be desired."

"Now, how?" demands Eaton, who has perhaps inherited some of his doggedness from her. If she had thought to subdue *him*, she too has been mistaken.

"Dear Eaton, I am not arguing with you. To argue with such a headstrong person is to know fatigue. I was merely making a remark to Mrs. Coventry."

"Oh! as for me," says Mrs. Coventry with a laugh, "I assure you I like the colonel immensely. He is one of the very few people with whom I can converse for half an hour without being bored to death."

"You are fortunate," says Lady Stamer, waving her fan slowly to and fro, and pretending to suppress a very superior smile.

"Still, my dear mother, you have not mentioned your objections to him," says Eaton.

"Mrs. Coventry has suggested your right line to you, Eaton," says Lady Stamer pleasantly. "You should have been an M.P. rather than a soldier; in the House you would have made yourself heard. I think if

I were a betting man I should back you liberally to reduce even the Irish members to silence, through sheer perseverance alone. As it is, you are completely thrown away."

"But about Colonel D'Arcy," says her son, with that persistency that has not endeared him to her. "You object to him. Why?"

"For many reasons. For every reason," with a touch of the temper that has hitherto been rigorously kept under control. "He is a person impossible to *place*, but as I regard him, he is positively insufferable. He says just what he chooses about most things, and has evidently no respect of persons."

"By which you mean that he speaks the truth in season and out of it. A curious accusation to bring against a son of Erin," says Eaton, with a mirth that is perhaps a trifle sardonic. "Where was he born, then, that he never came within touch of his Blarney Stone?"

"Where indeed! I am not his keeper," says Lady Stamer as pleasantly as ever, and as *un*pleasantly. "He may have travelled all over the known globe, so far as I know. What

I do know is, that he is brusque to a singular degree; and that all such people are better *out* of society than in it."

"What on earth can he have been saying about you?" says Mrs. Vaudrey. "I am afraid he has hopelessly offended you—but how? It must have been inadvertently, at all events. Perhaps he let out something that was in his mind without knowing it." This is highly suggestive, and leads Lady Stamer into even a more indignant frame of mind.

"Something against me?" says she with assumed cheerfulness. "Oh, that would be *too* amusing."

"It might be amusing, but one can't tell. Mistakes are often more embarrassing than truths. But you are so clever, you ought to know. Of course we can't know, but now if you were a person who could be rough, or proud, or could have behaved yourself frowardly towards him in any way, the situation might be understanded of the people. As it *is*, we all quite know how immaculate you are, and that therefore the quarrel cannot have been of your seeking."

This is nearly as terrible as Lady Stamer's descents upon her. There had been a day last year when Lady Stamer had gone to a local concert without remembering to remove from cheek and brow the tell-tale powder that lay thickly on them. It cost her many a *mauvais quart d'heure* afterwards, and her maid an excellent place, and the worst of it was, that not even these trials seemed to expiate the offence. It was not forgotten. Just now everybody seems to remember the little folly as freshly as though it had happened yesterday. Mrs. Vaudrey, angered by that uncivil allusion to her domestic difficulties, has avenged herself to a very satisfactory extent.

It is now Lady Stamer's turn to colour, slowly, but perceptibly.

"Certainly not of mine ; and as a fact there is no quarrel. I was merely saying that I do not think the D'Arcys good form. As for the girl, she is only a horrid little horse-breaker, no more."

"Something more, surely," says Eaton, who has grown rather white. "A very lovely and charming girl, for example."

"Oh, my dear Eaton, as for *you!*" says Lady Stamer with a shrug and a badly-suppressed bitterness of tone, "we cannot expect an unbiassed opinion from you; we know you are wedded to the family."

"Not yet, not *yet*," says Mr. Blount jovially, with a loud laugh, for which witticism he is rewarded by a stony stare from both mother and son.

"Some more tea, Bartholomew?" says Lady Stamer, in her most unpleasant tone. "No? Then perhaps you will ring for Mrs. Coventry's carriage. You look," severely, "as if you wanted something to do. So sorry you must go so soon," to Mrs. Coventry. "We hardly see anything of you now. Good-bye."

The others being prompt to follow Mrs. Coventry's lead, the drawing-room at Parklands is soon deserted.

CHAPTER XV

"It was absurd your inducing me to accept the invitation to the Castle," says Evelyn. "You must have known I couldn't go, after all. Cinderellas should stay at home, and not aspire to duchesses and such fal-lals. The sober walks of life are for them."

She is evidently in the last stage of depression. Sitting on a box that does duty for a chair, she looks up at Miss Vandeleur, with reproach in her eyes. Miss Vandeleur is sitting on the only available chair in Evelyn's bedroom; the other is sufficiently far gone in the disease called old age, to be found out by the most casual observer. It is indeed a rather decrepit room altogether. The little iron bedstead would have given way long ago if any other but the slender form of its owner had stepped into it. The looking-glass is ridiculously small, and tremulous at the hinges. The dressing-table is propped against the wall; the old wardrobe has a lock that would defy the ingenuity of any one except Evelyn to open or shut it. Everything is, however, scrupulously clean, and some flowers give it a friendly look. Its poor little mistress, looking the picture of despair, turns her eyes away from her visitor, and gives way to a deep sigh.

"You forget Cinderella changed her whole life by going to a ball, given not by a duchess, but by a prince," says Marian gaily. "I have set my heart on your having one good week."

"Well, but how? Do you think I am going in these rags?" pulling out a bit of her much-washed cotton frock, with a disgusted air. "To be laughed at by all the grandees. Not likely! And I could not ask the colonel for money just now."

"No?"

"Oh, no! I haven't said a word to any one," lowering her voice, "but of late he has seemed terribly depressed. Not *before* people, you will understand, but at home—with *us*. Both Jimmy and I have noticed it. Do you know he has grown quite irritable? He, who used to have such a lovely temper."

"But how do you account for it?"

"I'm not sure about it," hesitating, "but I think it is something about money."

Miss Vandeleur makes an impatient movement.

"It always *is*," she says.

"I can't quite make it out," says Evelyn in a puzzled way, a frown wrinkling her smooth forehead. "But I think he gave money to Major Arthurs. You remember him, don't you? A queer sort of man who used to live down at that house just outside Fenton. He was there all last autumn."

"Of course I remember," gravely; "he gave him money, you say. But I did not think the colonel could—had—that he——"

"No, he couldn't, of course. He never has a penny to spare, poor darling; but he put his name to some paper——"

"Oh!" says Miss Vandeleur; she stops short and looks at Evelyn. "But Major Arthurs we always thought was a man who had plenty of money."

" The colonel thought so too," says Evelyn ruefully. " He doesn't think so *now*. At all events, however it was, he asked the colonel to lend him some money, and the colonel did it. He can't say no to any one."

" A great pity. He backed some bills for him, I suppose?"

" Yes, that is it," eagerly, as if helped out of a difficulty. " It is the same thing, isn't it?"

" Worse, far worse!" says Miss Vandeleur, with a very concerned air.

" Well, that's what he did," says Evelyn.

About this time last year, or perhaps a month or two later, Major Arthurs had dropped down upon Fenton as if from the clouds.

He had, however, brought with him a considerable amount of information about himself, and references to relations or friends of theirs in the neighbourhood ; to say nothing of an excellent hunting stud, a groom, a helper, and all the usual signs of being comfortably off, if not actually wealthy.

He had just retired from the army ; why,

most satisfactorily explained. He had distant connections who were known, by name at least, to all at Fenton; perhaps not sufficiently well known to be put down on their correspondence list, but still known; and after all, one can write at any moment even to the commonest stranger, and get an answer too, if occasion arises for it.

He was a youngish man, who might have been thirty and probably was forty; with a manner so gay, so *insouciant*, so genuine, that soon he was a general favourite in Fenton.

At Parklands he had been made specially welcome, his mother (who luckily for her was dead for many years) having been a cousin and a great friend of Lady Stamer's.

To Colonel D'Arcy, this dropper in upon his stupidity had been a perfect godsend. He had welcomed him as such after a first delightful interview, during which Major Arthurs had displayed such a knowledge of horseflesh as should encharm the soul of any Irishman.

As a fact he really *did* understand horses. He was, too, a genial man in conversation;

never self-assertive, never unduly obstinate, always willing to concede a touchy point; always ready to smooth the angularity of a troublesome corner. He was indeed of so gay and of so harmonious a disposition that rich and poor alike paid him court; and one poor Irishman in particular was brought to great straits because of him.

No one knew how it began; the colonel himself being always rather hazy about it. But at all events he induced the colonel to put his name to several bills for him, always protesting in his lightest, airiest manner, that it was but a matter of the moment only. Indeed, so well appointed was the well-connected man that the colonel felt the sort of worldly pleasure in helping the rich that we all do.

The last bill had been signed in January, a six months' bill, and almost directly afterwards the genial man had disappeared. He had bidden the neighbourhood generally a good-bye for a week or two. He was going to London on Friday—could he do any commissions? He would be back on Monday. This to the women. He had even pressed the colonel to

come up to town with him, knowing, perhaps,
that the colonel never had money to fritter
away upon trips of any sort.

He had gone to London—or to the other
place—but he had certainly not come back
on Monday, or any other day. Indeed he
never came back at all.

Though to show he was not a common villain who might be a disgrace to this mild
book, let it be known at once that his references were quite correct ; that he was related
to so and so ; that his mother was Lady
Stamer's cousin ; but that, in spite of all
these claims to respectability, he was an un-
mitigated blackguard, who had been kicked
out of the army and every club to which he
had belonged for cheating ; and was now
merely a beast of prey, roaming the earth in
search of some such easy prey as Colonel
D'Arcy.

All this might have been matter of comment, and might have prevented many im-
portant and sad events in Fenton, if somebody had taken the precaution to write a line
or two about him to those people whom he

had, with the boldness of the successful swindler, given as his referees.

The colonel was the victim ; but for a long time he had remained blind to his situation. He had indeed thought nothing of the unpleasant position in which he stood, until a note from the manager of the local bank, saying the first bill was due, roused within him a faint touch of anxiety as to where Arthurs was. He wrote to the club address that Arthurs had given him, but got no answer. He wrote again, and was informed that Major Arthurs had taken his name off the books two years ago. He then wrote to his home address, where the man's father was popularly supposed to be living, and received in return a post-card from the housekeeper, to say Major Arthurs had not been there for eighteen months, and that she had no idea where he was at present.

All this was very discouraging. Colonel D'Arcy was conscious of a slight feeling of alarm, but disliking unpleasant sensations of all sorts thrust it determinedly into the background. He took the whole affair indeed with extraordinary phlegm, until the second bill fell due, and was forthwith protested.

Then a doubt that Arthurs must be dead first filled his breast, and that, if so, it might prove awkward for him—Colonel D'Arcy. It was not indeed until his wife, who sometimes had glimpses of common sense, suggested to him that, possibly, Arthurs might have been an accomplished swindler, that the full meaning of the injury that had been done him awoke within his breast.

If this thing was true—why, then—— He could not follow out the thought; in one little second, it seemed to him, he was by many years an older man; but he *had* to face it out. Why, *then*—he was a pauper, and his children beggars.

It was a bitter moment. All that he had would scarcely suffice to meet the unjust debt. His house, his few acres, his furniture, his horses—that were his principal means of living —that last young colt, that looked as if he was capable of so many things—all must go. His heart contracted with a cruel pang as he thought of that young colt.

Yet it, and every one of his worldly possessions, would scarcely suffice to satisfy this claim upon him. *Two thousand pounds!* Dropping into a chair, he wondered vaguely how he could ever have been capable of letting himself in for so outrageous a piece of folly.

"Evelyn," says Miss Vandeleur, getting up from the reliable chair and seating herself on the half of Evelyn's box, "it is, as you say, impossible that you should now trouble your uncle about money matters. It is equally impossible that you should refuse the duchess's invitation. In fact you *must* go to the Castle, and as for your clothes, I'll see about that."

"Oh, *no*," flushing hotly.

"Don't try to be conventional," says Miss Vandeleur calmly. "There is no necessity for it, between you and me, and I know all you think you ought to say, and the absurdity of it. I am as fond of you as if you were my sister, and if I have money and you haven't, there is no reason on earth why I shouldn't give you some of mine. If you were rich and I was poor, I shouldn't hesitate for a moment to——"

"Say no to me for my kind offer," inter rupts Evelyn, with a little curious laugh.

"I hope you are not going to be trouble- some about this matter, Evelyn," says Miss Vandeleur in a rather vexed tone. "Supposed dignity very often comes under the head of folly. If I thought you should not accept my offer, believe me, I should never have made it; and," with a milder glance, "I *thought* we were such great friends."

"So we are! so we are," cries Evelyn, softened at once by the reproach in her friend's eyes. "And I shouldn't mind a bit letting you give me a frock, only—there's the colonel, you see—*he* would not like it either."

The "either" is a slip, and tells her real feelings.

"As little as you would, you mean."

"I don't think I meant that," restlessly.

"No?" wisely refraining from pressing this point. "Then if it is only the colonel—why should he know?"

"It might be hidden from him, of course," with downcast eyes and dejected mien. "But

—I should feel so horrid about keeping it secret from him; you see, here, in this house, we tell each other everything."

" A well-regulated household!" says Marian laughing. "Nonsense, however! If it comes to that, *I'll* tell the colonel all about it, and you'll see he will let me have my own way in spite of you." She turns the girl's face lightly towards hers and scans it with kindly scrutiny. "I should have more trouble to gain your consent to my scheme than the colonel's," says she shrewdly.

" Oh, how you misjudge me," says Evelyn, with a disgraceful, but useless, attempt at subterfuge; she draws her face away from the other's gentle touch, and smiles nervously. Miss Vandeleur, as if a little puzzled, waits a minute or so, and then slightly changes the conversation.

" I shall feel absolutely friendless if you won't come," she says. " I shall be almost alone, and duchesses, being rare, are oppressive. If we were *together*, we might enjoy ourselves, and Eaton Stamer is to be there and his brother." She throws in the brother as though Sir Bertram is a person of small account.

"Yes, I know," says Evelyn. She is twisting her handkerchief round and round her first finger as if her whole soul is bent on bandaging that slender member. But now, quite suddenly, she lifts her head and looks at Marian.

"Do you know what I heard a few days ago?" says she, speaking with singular distinctness. "That Lady Stamer is very anxious that you should marry Eaton."

"Is she?" says Miss Vandeleur. She bursts out laughing, yet a crimson flush dyes her cheek and brow. "People often show most anxiety about things that they cannot bring to pass."

"You mean—— ?" leaning forward.

"That Eaton will not ask me to marry him."

"Only that?"

"Why—if you will have it," says Marian, laughing again—"though it is a thing a woman should not say until the opportunity has been given her of proving the truth of her words—I certainly do not want to marry Eaton."

"Ah!" says the girl quickly. Then—as if crushed by some fear—she lets her eyes fall, and her fingers fasten closely in the handkerchief that has now become a mere little round ball. "It—I thought it would have been rather a nice marriage," says she confusedly.

"According to your own showing, you and Lady Stamer are for once agreed," says Marian lightly. She understands it all quite well now, and resolves to return to her effort to take the girl with her to the Castle. "I am sorry I must disappoint all your hopes. But then—you have disappointed mine. Evelyn, change your mind. I am sure you would enjoy your week at the Castle."

"Oh, I should like it," her face now bright and irresolute. "But—would there be time?"

"To get a frock or two? Of course! I could telegraph to town. We could get down the skirts, ready made, from Black's, and you know Marsden is excellent so far as a body goes. She will fit you and follow out all our directions. It is now"—glancing at her

watch—"two o'clock. If I telegraph at once
we could get them down by the last train."

"Do you think I ought to go?" says
Evelyn, still hesitating. It is the last faint
protest, and is altogether different from the
hesitation of a while ago.

"*Pouf!*" says Marian contemptuously.
"Get up and help me to write the telegram;
time is flying."

"Oh, I'm *glad* I'm going," cries Evelyn presently, when a messenger has been dispatched
with the telegram. She throws her arms
round Marian and gives her what the children
call a "bear's hug." "I do so want to see a
little bit of life before I die. And I want too
—to make Lady Stamer *mad.*"

"That's being honestly vindictive," says
Marian. "Poor Lady Stamer, I often think
she is more to be pitied than anybody."

"I don't pity her. I shouldn't dream of
wasting so good a feeling on her. See how
she behaves to Eaton. All her affection is
given to Sir Bertram."

"And he, I'm afraid, doesn't care for her,"
in a low tone.

"That is only mere justice. However, he can manage very well for himself. He has not so much feeling as Eaton."

"You are quite mistaken there," says Miss Vandeleur, with a sudden and unexpected warmth. "Because he is so silent, people think he is phlegmatic—but they are mistaken."

"You seem to have studied him," says Evelyn curiously.

"Most people are interesting to me," says Marian calmly. "I like to think them out." She has quite recovered her usual mild manner. "And, after all, I don't see what great difference Lady Stamer makes between her two sons."

"Oh! Then you are the only one who *doesn't* see it. She adores Sir Bertram, and treats Eaton abominably."

"What!" laughing; "*you* can say that? You, who tell me she is bent on givin him—me!"

"Well, that puzzles me certainly. I wonder," says Evelyn thoughtfully, "why it hasn't occurred to her to give you to Sir Bertram."

"*Evelyn!*" says Miss Vandeleur with a sharpness, an involuntary movement, that startles the younger girl.

"Why," says she, "I——"

"Oh, no, it was nothing," interrupts Miss Vandeleur quickly. "Only—you must not talk to me—like that—about Lady Stamer! She wouldn't like it. Nobody would. And as for Sir Bertram——"

"She won't hear of it," says Evelyn; "she can't. I never said it to any one before."

"I hope not," earnestly, and looking with a rather pale face at her companion. "Promise me more, that you will not ever say it again."

"I promise," in a rather wondering tone. "But—— Oh," looking out of the window, "here is Eaton coming across the lawn, and Batty" (Mr. Blount's pet name) "and—Mr. Crawford. Come down and help me to talk to them."

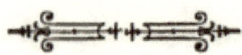

CHAPTER XVI

" HERE we are!" cries Mr. Blount cheerfully, as the girls enter the drawing-room. He is always terribly cheerful. " Eaton and I were coming up to have a look at you, when we met Mr. Crawford. We asked him to give us the light of his countenance. Whatever we are, *he* looks respectable. So we thought if he took us in tow we might present a better appearance."

" Against every word of that speech I enter a protest," says Captain Stamer.

" So do I," says Mr. Crawford. " It is most unfair that he should give you the impression that he induced me to come here. I assure you, Miss D'Arcy, I was within your gates, with the design of calling upon—Mrs. D'Arcy, when Mr. Blount met me."

" Tut," says she, with a tilt of her pretty chin, " who minds Batty!" Whereupon that

young man turns on her a glance replete with
reproach.

"You know I am defenceless when in your
presence, Evelyn," says he mournfully.

"And a good thing too," says she, "for if
you had a sword, *I* certainly would be the one
to draw it—not you.   And after that, the consequences to you would probably be awful."

"She's not well to-day," says Mr. Blount in
a generous aside.   "One can see that.   Well,
a truce to hostilities.   What we principally
came for was to know who is, and who is not,
going to the Castle next week."

"We are," says Marian Vandeleur, includ-
ing Evelyn in the " we " by a slight gesture.

"Oh! you are going, then," says Captain
Stamer, addressing Evelyn.   He had evidently
had doubts about it.

"Yes; Marian has persuaded me," says she
rather shamefacedly.   Perhaps after all she
should not have accepted those pretty gowns.
A cloud steals over her face.

"Then we are all going," says Mr. Blount.
"That throws a roseate hue over the fact that
we shall have to koo-too to a live duchess for

seven long days. The tribe is so very nearly extinct that we approach it with reverence and awe."

"You, too, are to be one of the duchess's guests?" asks Evelyn, smiling at Mr. Crawford.

"No. I am not so fortunate," replies he, smiling in return, as though he finds it impossible to resist her; as if, too, smiles are strangers to him. "I am sorry *now* I was not introduced to her. She might have asked me." The implied compliment is very delicately tendered.

"Oh! I am sorry," says the girl very gently, and with something of sincerity in her tone. She is leaning forward and looking up at him, with parted lips, and eyes that smile at him through lids half lowered. That she *is* really a little sorry because he cannot be one of her companions at the Castle is quite clear. Only a little sorry, truly—but how much even a crumb is to a starving soul.

"I say," says Mr. Blount to Evelyn, with a sprightly laugh, "you should have seen my aunt's face when she heard you were going to

the Castle. Green isn't the colour. It was
ever so many shades deeper than that. No
love lost between you two, eh?"

A deadly silence follows this pleasing remark. A quick red flush mounts to Evelyn's
brow, an angry flush, and she straightens her
pretty figure and throws up her head in a
rather militant fashion. Miss Vandeleur bends
over a bunch of Dijon roses, and seeks for
comfort there. Stamer, looking at the culprit, explains all too fully by his glance that
it would give him keen pleasure to drop him
by the nape of the neck into the garden below.

The entrance of Mrs. D'Arcy is felt by
everybody, save one, to be a special interven-
tion of Providence. In a body they rise to
greet her. She is, indeed, received with an
enthusiasm that possibly puzzles her.

Evelyn alone remains unmoved.

"I hate her!" says she, with the prompt
and terrible downrightness that belongs to
youth alone.

"Who, dear?" asks Mrs. D'Arcy, pausing
in her smiling vivacious journey up the room.

"There is only one person," says Evelyn

with a little shrug — "*you* know! Lady Stamer."

"Oh, nonsense!" says Mrs. D'Arcy, with an apologetic glance at Eaton.

"Yes, I do. I can't *bear* her," persists Evelyn mutinously, in spite of a second warning glance from Marian, who too would have her bear in mind the presence of Lady Stamer's son.

"Dear Evelyn!" says she in a very low tone. But the lowest tone in a small room is generally the property of all.

"I know," says the girl promptly. "It doesn't matter. He understands. I've often told him how I hate her. You aren't offended, Eaton, are you? And she hates *me*. She is as velvety as a cat to other people, but she looks at me like *this*," closing her lovable eyes, and caricaturing Lady Stamer's put-on hauteur to perfection.

"I don't think, Evelyn, you ought to speak of Lady Stamer like that," says Mrs. D'Arcy, making her protest plainly through a sense of duty, that is utterly destroyed by the fact that she is laughing immoderately.

"No?　Why?" demands Evelyn with a tilt of her chin.　"Because she happens to be my enemy?　Oh, that is too hard a doctrine for ordinary people.　And besides, even in little ways she is aggravating.　She," looking round suddenly to where Mr. Crawford is sitting, as though sure of getting sympathy from him, "always gives my name only *two* syllables. She calls me Eve-lyn, *so*," with a nod of her small head.　"As though I were the mother of all living.　In Ireland we hate to hear the name pronounced like that."

"She's a criminal!" says Mr. Blount.　"She oughtn't to be let loose on society.　What are the police about?"

"And I like to be called Ev-e-lyn, *so*," goes on Miss D'Arcy, very properly taking no heed of him.

"Evelyn, *so!*" repeats Captain Stamer, in a little mocking tone, that is a very successful imitation of hers.

"Evelyn, so, so," says Mr. Blount quite affectionately.

"*Evelyn!*" says Mr. Crawford.

It is so sudden a pronunciation of her name

—there is something so passionate yet so de-
spairing in the sound of it—that involuntarily
everybody grows still and looks at Mr. Crawford. He has spoken from out the gloom of
the falling curtains, and his voice is startling
because of its strange intensity. It is as
though the man has forgotten that any one is
within these four walls, save he himself, and
the bearer of that charmed name. Perhaps,
indeed, for the moment he has even forgotten
her bodily presence.

There is something tragic in his utterance
that reveals to all present the secret of his
heart—all save one: That one is Evelyn.

"Eh?" says she, as though indeed he had
called to her. She turns her expressive face
to his, as though waiting for an answer. For
the second she is dead to the thought that he
certainly would not address her by her Christian name, and looks at him expectantly as
though he had actually called to her—as in
truth he has, *unconsciously*, from out the empti-
ness of his soul.

But no answer comes to her vague inquiry.
Mr. Crawford, as if not knowing that any

word had escaped him or her, sits motionless, the absent look that usually characterizes his face now strongly pronounced. It is an inward gaze, that repulses the many and raises pity in the few. Evelyn still leans forward, fascinated by that strange stare, and waiting for the answer—that will never come.

There threatens to be a very awkward pause, when suddenly Mr. Blount comes to the rescue.

" *Quite* so! " says he promptly, addressing Crawford, whom indeed he is regarding with a delighted eye. To him Crawford is a man rich in promise. Anything so *naïve*, so fresh, has seldom come within his knowledge. To be in love is one thing; to betray one's love so nobly to all the world is quite another; and to give a " private view " of it to one's friends, as Crawford has just done, is a novelty indeed, and almost more than need be expected even in this ingenuous age.

Mr. Blount is conscious that he is enjoying himself thoroughly, and that he has by no means wasted a day in coming to Firgrove. Not only Crawford but his cousin seem full of possibilities. Eaton, sitting over there, with an eye fixed on Crawford, and with murder in that eye, is a feast in itself.

"You like my name?" says Evelyn at last, getting no direct answer from Crawford, and being anxious to hear somebody's voice again.

"Yes," says Mr. Crawford slowly, like one awakening from a dream. A hideous dream, if one may judge by the wildness of the eyes he now raises to Evelyn's face. Whatever his thoughts have been during the past three minutes, wherever they have flown, no man need envy them!

"You can see at once that it is a prettier name with three syllables than with two," goes on Evelyn in her little friendly way, still addressing him, as if that strange expression of his is unknown to her.

"We all know it is the dearest name in the world," says Captain Stamer unexpectedly, and with something of the vehemence of anger in his tone; he is smiling, however, as he speaks; and as he ceases he laughs—rather nervously. Of late he always laughs when attempting to pay Evelyn a compliment. A

tincture of fear has mingled itself with his
friendliness towards her. To Evelyn it seems
as though he is ever bent on turning what
might be reality into jest, and the thought
puzzles her. It is at such moments as these
that she understands him least—is least at
touch with him; perhaps because it is that
at such unreal periods he does not understand
himself.

"Those poor people you have been so kind
to, Mr. Crawford—they are so grateful," says
Mrs. D'Arcy, beaming upon the silent man
with an admiration not to be subdued. "Mr.
Vaudrey has been telling me all about it—
that poor boy, he is really on the road to re-
covery, I hear. What a blessing to his poor
mother—and to his benefactor too," with another smile and a little nod—"a blessing that
will come home, I don't doubt."

"It is nothing, nothing," says Mr. Crawford
hastily, crossing the room to her side, in a
certain speedy fashion that suggests the idea
of his being anxious to lower her tone. "Mr.
Vaudrey has done everything. I have been
glad to be his helper."

" You would play second fiddle," says she, as if amused. " Why, that is a *rôle* that all men refuse. No, no, you must wear your blushing honours as thick as you have woven them. The song of praise will be sounded in your ears, whether you will or no."

" Lamentations, it should be," says he in a low tone. Then, " You have been very kind to me so far, Mrs. D'Arcy," says he, with his eyes on the ground. " You can, if you will, even add to that kindness. Never again give me credit for any charitable act."

" Oh! but that is supreme modesty," says she lightly. " It is almost affectation. In reality, though one disclaims the desire for praise, one feels aggrieved if the praise is not given. You must not prove yourself super-latively good, or you will be unpopular in Fenton."

" I shall not be proved unpopular on that count," returns he slowly.

"Well, I don't know, you bid fair for it. There is Evelyn, she is almost as bad as the rector in her admiration of your charities."

" Miss D'Arcy is charity personified if she

can think thus of me. But I do not dare to believe she thinks of me at all. As for charity, it has its being under so many hundred names that the real true charity is hard to find."

"Love is the best name of all," says Mrs. D'Arcy.

"Ah!" He pauses, and looks down again. "To be truly charitable, then, you believe one should love the object of one's charity?"

"Oh, no, not that exactly; charity would be an easy virtue if that were so. But one should love to give where necessity calls for giving; and one should not look for gain to self *in* that giving, whether from earth or heaven."

Mr. Crawford lifts his eyes, and studies her face for a moment with a certain intentness. And now he sighs and turns aside.

"How gently you can deal a death-blow," says he. "But a truce to all such arguments; they are sickly, dull, and slow; you must pardon my introduction of them."

"Of charity! that sweetest of all gifts——"

"Let us talk of something else," says he with determination. "Of—your niece, for example."

"Of Evelyn? Almost as sweet a topic," says Mrs. D'Arcy genially. "I'm glad you like her." To Mrs. D'Arcy, who is still young, it seems quite natural to speak without reserve of so young a girl as Evelyn to this man, who may well come under the category of old.

"Everybody likes her, I suppose. It is a paltry word," says Mr. Crawford.

"Yes; *most* people, at all events. You can see for yourself how lovable she is—so bright, so pretty. You think her pretty?"

"That too is a paltry word," says he smiling. "Surely—like the flowers or the birds—she is lovely."

"She is—she is!" with open delight. "*You* understand her. She is the sunshine of this house; I'm sure how I—how the children—could get on without her, I haven't the courage to work out; and as for Colonel D'Arcy, he adores her."

"And yet," says Mr. Crawford thoughtfully, "there have been moments when I have seen the gaiety fade from her face, and a shadow replace it; I——" he pauses with a touch of confusion curious in so quiet a man. "I have watched her. I am a student of human nature, you will see; and the changes in her nature, from sunshine to gloom at intervals, have, I confess, interested me."

" As for that," says Mrs. D'Arcy, with a half glance to where Evelyn is standing at the end of the room trying to put a spider down Mr. Blount's back, "she often puzzles *me*. But there are reasons for those sudden changes in her—many, indeed, but one that overtops all the others. The few I can name, but that other we never speak about; she has made us promise silence. You will hear her discussed often, but you must not mind all that people say."

" I shall mind nothing."

" She has had a sad life. As I think I told you before she was made an orphan when still very young. Her mother died in giving her birth; her father, who was an old man when she was born, he—well, well, it is a sad story, Mr. Crawford, and one we seldom dwell on. We never talk of it—at all events before her."

Mr. Crawford inclines his head sympathetically. "Father a scoundrel, did something disreputable," is his swift inward comment on her words, to be followed as swiftly by a bitter self-accusation. Who is he that he should condemn any man—call any man a sinner!

"Yes, yes," goes on Mrs. D'Arcy meditatively. "She has had some griefs—great griefs. But she is, as I have said, the sunshine of this house for all that. She has," with a stifled sigh, "little lovable ways of her own that can cheer and comfort when most things fail." This last terrible trouble of the colonel's comes home to her as she speaks, and with it the knowledge of how Evelyn has striven to lessen it, and give hope to him, and not only to him but to her likewise.

"It is an easy matter to believe in the beauty of your niece's nature," says Mr. Crawford in his slow, methodical fashion.

FIVE long days, oppressively warm, inconceivably monotonous, have at last buried themselves, with a reluctance, and a most indecent determination to make the most of the time allotted them; and now at last the greater number of those we know are assembled on the lawn of Carminster Castle. To-day is Tuesday; to-morrow July will be a week old.

Already, as we see at every glance around, summer is well advanced, and soon autumn will be with us. But who cares for that so long as the sun is shining, and flowers blooming, and life, not death, is present? A fig for those pessimistic ones who, forgetting the joys of the moment, look forward only to the sorrows of the future. To be morbid is to be an ungrateful fool. "Sufficient unto the day," says the greatest authority of all, " is the evil thereof."

To-day is one of July's gayest efforts. It is

so mild, so balmy, so full of perfumes delicately mixed and mingled, that the vaunted air that is popularly supposed to blow so " soft o'er Ceylon's Isle " is but a distant cousin to it ; not even a near relation.

The different groups spread abroad over the terraces, lawns, and tennis courts, are all either gasping with heat, or sitting languidly beneath wide white umbrellas, wondering why on earth they are not indoors behind the kindly blinds that are bidding defiance to old Sol.

" I shan't live through it," says Evelyn, who has cast herself upon a long garden seat somewhat in the shade, after giving her opponents a terrible beating at the last game. " How do I look, Batty ? " to Mr. Blount. " Boiled ? —roasted ? "

" That's just like girls ! " says Mr. Blount, who is cross because he is too warm. " They keep on hinting and hinting in the meanest fashion, when they might just as well speak out at once. All the world knows that you want me to say you are as pale as the driven snow, in spite of the day being at——"

" I want nothing of the kind," says Miss

D'Arcy indignantly. "Really, Bartholomew, I think it would be an advantage to you if you——"

"Were a little less candid and honest-spoken," supplies Mr. Blount promptly. "I agree with you. The ingenuousness of my speech very often——"

"Ingenuity you mean," scornfully.

"That's an old trick, you know," says Mr. Blount. "Any one could do that. Most wards can be twisted, but nothing can finally crush the *Truth*, in large capitals. And, as I have just said, girls are all regular born Isaac Waltons. Fishing for compliments is their forte."

"What's yours? Shall I tell you?" Miss D'Arcy is beginning with fell design in her eye, when luckily the duchess strolling up to her puts a semicolon at all events to her next remark.

"I must congratulate you on that last game," says she, smiling at Evelyn, who is accounted very pretty and out of the common run by her. "Mrs. Weekling-Wylde was quite crushed."

"Yes?" says Evelyn hesitating, and looking a little puzzled. As well she may. She
has not often heard Mrs. Wylding-Weekes thus
named. But the duchess has quite a talent
for forgetting little trifles such as names,
dates, &c.

"Mrs. Weekling-Wylde is a mere amateur
when compared with Miss D'Arcy," says Mr.
Blount with astounding gravity. He drops a
supernaturally grave wink on Evelyn as he says
this, which she openly resents. The duchess,
needless to say, is looking the other way.

Her whole attention indeed is given to the
advancing figure of a man, whom, as she tells
herself, she is unable instantly to place. It is
the weekly day she has set apart to receive
the county generally, and it is a point of
honour with her to be able to remember any
one with whom she has had even five minutes'
conversation. Mrs. Wylding-Weekes, who
arrived an hour ago, was received with effusion, the duchess being under the impression
that she was the wife of a county mag-
nate in the neighbourhood, an M.P., and a
man of some notoriety who has made himself

specially obnoxious over the Irish question, and who is therefore a sort of person to be trotted out and interviewed. It was only indeed when she asked the astonished Mr. Wylding-Weekes what he *really* meant to do for "the poor dear Irish," that the mistake transpired.

Far from being discouraged, however, the duchess, who is in her most genial mood, now looks out afar for fresh material on which to expend her overflowing *bonhomie.*

"Who's the death's-head?" asks she, demanding an answer from Mr. Blount who is nearest to her, but with her eyes on Mr. Crawford, who is slowly making his way towards her across the shaven lawn.

Bartholomew, thus addressed, pours forth explanations to her under his breath.

"Crawford. The Grange. New-comer. Got the 'dyspepsy.' Doesn't know what's good for him. Too much money. One of those 'poor rich men' somebody speaks of. Looks as if he didn't know what to do with his superfluous coppers. Wish *I* was in the way of giving him a lead!"

" Well, why don't you ? " asks the duchess.

" Haven't got the tin," says Mr. Blount, with a noble candour that is only to be outdone by the simplicity of his elegance.

The duchess receives Mr. Crawford in her most gracious style. He may be solemn, he is undoubtedly difficult, but the man's a man for a' that.

"Such *perfect* weather," says she, smiling amiably. She is still young, and the responsibilities of her position have ever been sealed books to her. She would have made an excellent wife for a country squire, and indeed for the matter of that she had been an excellent wife to the late duke, who had adored her.

" The best summer we have had for years," says she in her exuberant fashion, beaming on Crawford. Unlike other folk, she always begins with the weather. It is safe. The condition of the atmosphere is therefore a marked feature in her conversation. " *What* a sun ! I don't believe India can be warmer!" This is a stock phrase. In winter she alters it by, "I don't believe the North Pole can be colder."

"It means rain, I think," says Mr. Crawford. This is, or át least should be, a damper, but duchesses are never damped.

"You *really* think so? I don't. No, no, those clouds over there mean nothing but perpetual heat." She doesn't want to explain this remarkable prognostication. "The whole look of the afternoon reminds me of that delightful day at Lady Stamer's, where we first met. As I was saying to you then, I think this part of the county is the driest in England."

As she had said nothing to him at Parklands about the county or anything else—for the simple reason that she had not even seen him there—this is a slightly embarrassing speech. Mr. Blount is enchanted by it, and stands by waiting eagerly for a *dénouement* that may add to his delight—but disappointment alone awaits him. Mr. Crawford bows politely, and passes it over, whereupon Mr. Blount falls back on Evelyn with a disgusted countenance.

"Just what 1 always thought. Man's a perfect hypocrite," says he indignantly.

"Do you play tennis, Mr. Rockfort?" asks the duchess pleasantly of Crawford. "No? What a pity! Well, you know everybody here, I daresay, better than I do. And here is Miss D'Arcy unattached; will you take that seat near her?"

She smiles kindly and moves away, whilst Mr. Crawford, taking her hint with alacrity, drops into the seat next Evelyn.

END OF VOL. I.

PRINTED BY
KELLY AND CO., MIDDLE MILL, KINGSTON-ON-THAMES
AND GATE STREET, LINCOLN'S INN FIELDS, W.C.

www.ingramcontent.com/pod-product-compliance
Lightning Source LLC
Chambersburg PA
CBHW030817020726
47499CB00006B/1963